D0711744

Dear Reader,

Thank you so much for picking up *Real Men Wear Plaid!*
This book holds a special place in my heart because
the idea for it was conceived during a trip to Scotland
with fellow writers and friends. (Check them out at
the writingplayground.com.) I absolutely loved the
country—the lochs and mountains, the shaggy Highland
cows, the thistle and sheep. And the history… I felt like I
was breathing it in as we visited all the castles and ruins.
I couldn't think of a better place to set my first Blaze
Encounters. I also couldn't come up with any sexier men.

But these guys aren't just hot—they're brothers!
Ewan MacKinnon finds the woman of his dreams
wandering on the West Highland Way. Cam MacKinnon's
soul mate blows him away at a murder mystery weekend
at his Highland castle. And Alec MacKinnon meets his
match when his mentor's daughter takes up residence in
his seaside town.

Nothing brings a smile to my face faster than hearing
from my readers, so be sure to check out my website
at ReadRhondaNelson.com. Also, the Blaze authors
have just started up a cool Pet Project. Be sure to visit
blazeauthors.com to see what we're up to and how you
can help.

Happy reading!

Rhonda

Rhonda Nelson

REAL MEN WEAR PLAID!

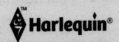

TORONTO NEW YORK LONDON
AMSTERDAM PARIS SYDNEY HAMBURG
STOCKHOLM ATHENS TOKYO MILAN MADRID
PRAGUE WARSAW BUDAPEST AUCKLAND

Recycling programs
for this product may
not exist in your area.

ISBN-13: 978-0-373-79619-9

REAL MEN WEAR PLAID!

Copyright © 2011 by Rhonda Nelson

www.Harlequin.com

Printed in U.S.A.

ABOUT THE AUTHOR

A Waldenbooks bestselling author, two-time RITA® Award nominee and *RT Book Reviews* Reviewers' Choice nominee, Rhonda Nelson writes hot romantic comedy for the Harlequin Blaze line and other Harlequin imprints. With more than twenty-five published books to her credit and many more coming down the pike, she's thrilled with her career and enjoys dreaming up her characters and manipulating the worlds they live in. As well as a writing career, she has a husband, two adorable kids, a black Lab and a beautiful bichon frise. She and her family make their chaotic but happy home in a small town in northern Alabama. She loves to hear from her readers, so be sure and check her out at www.ReadRhondaNelson.com.

Books by Rhonda Nelson

To my Scotland travel buddies.
Most specifically to Kim, for all her planning, wonderful in-laws, her car *and* her ability to drive on the wrong side of the road.
To Kira, for the unforgettable horseback riding excursion across the Highlands. (You know I didn't type that with a straight face.) To Andrea, the ultimate navigator who made sure we were never lost. And to Danniele, who patted my back while I emptied my full Scottish breakfast onto the sidewalk a block off the Royal Mile.

THE WANDERER

Prologue

GENEVIEVE MACKINNON OFTEN marveled over the fact that brilliance and stupidity could occupy the same body—the same mind—and a perfect example of that phenomenon was seated at the desk in front of her.

"Sons," her father, Hamish MacKinnon, railed for what felt like the upteenth time. "I've got three of them—*three*," he repeated, as if she weren't aware of how many brothers she had. "And not one of them willing to take on MacKinnon Holdings so that I can retire properly with your mother and spend our golden years fly fishing and vacationing in Majorca."

Genevieve dutifully handed over another paper that required her father's signature. She cast a glance out the window, observing passersby three floors below in Edinburgh proper. "I wasn't aware that Mother wanted to take up fly-fishing," she said mildly, her lips twitching with humor.

Her father shot her an impatient look. "You know very well what I mean," he told her. "I'm sixty-five. It's time for me to enjoy the fruits of my labor, to hand over the reins. With three sons at my disposal I never worried about not being able to pass the torch, as it were." He grimaced, his face settling into one of heart-breaking disappointment. "Instead I've spent my life building a family business that none of them seems to want."

Genevieve wished that she could disagree, but her father was right. Her brothers—Ewan, Cam and Alec—were all either carving their own path, or in Ewan's case, still looking for it, and weren't the least inclined to continue along the road their father had built.

They weren't…but she was and always had been.

Pity that her father didn't see it.

She handed him another document and inwardly sighed. How much harder could she work? How many hours must she log in before he realized that *his* company was *her* life, the only one she'd ever wanted? She was in her element at MacKinnon Holdings, had a knack for making good investments and had a better understanding of the business world than any of her dear brothers ever would. And yet they were better qualified in her father's eyes because they had a penis? Ridiculous. Utter stupidity.

"Marshall Anderson will be here at one," she said, trying to get a handle on her temper.

Her father's keen eyes instantly found hers. "You're ready for him, I presume?"

"I've reviewed the past ten years' financials, interviewed all pertinent staff—" not to mention the nonsalaried workers, who tended to give a better picture of a man's character "—and am confident that the company is sound. It is not, however, worth what he wants us to pay for it."

"Then I'll leave the negotiations to you," he said. "I'm meeting your mother for lunch."

She nodded, presuming as much. He often "left things to her" yet seemed inexplicably reluctant to leave her in charge of the company.

"Don't worry, Genevieve," he said, sending her an indulgent smile. "At some point one of your brothers has to come round and when they do, I won't depend on you so much."

Could he hear the enamel grinding off her teeth? she wondered as it resonated through her own ears. Not trusting herself to speak, she merely managed a weak smile and left the office.

Obviously a talk with her brothers was going to be in order.

1

"SOME BEST friend," Gemma Wentworth muttered between clenched teeth.

He'd left her? Here? In the wilds of Scotland, a little over half-way along the famous West Highland Way?

Gemma felt the impact of what he'd done fully smack into her. She stared at the young Irish couple who'd delivered his message.

"Are you certain?" she asked faintly. Her stomach gave a sickening little pitch. "You saw him leave?"

The girl nodded sympathetically. "We did. He climbed right into the lorry and took off, he did."

But—but she'd only gone to the bathroom, Gemma thought, her mind gauzy with shock. She turned toward the little store, then scanned the parking lot and surrounding area just to make sure that Jeffrey—her oldest and dearest friend—wasn't going to magically appear.

"He said to give you this," the guy chimed in, handing her Jeffrey's backpack. It felt lighter, meaning he'd taken his clothes and pounds of grooming products. Her friend was more particular about his appearance than she was, the great jerk. "Said he wouldn't need it anymore and that…he was sorry," the young man finished, evidently finding the message and the words distasteful.

Sorry? Anger bullied the initial shock aside as she considered what he'd done to her. *Sorry?* She gave a grim laugh. Oh, he'd be sorry all right. What sort of friend abandoned another so-called best friend without so much as a goodbye *in the middle of a foreign country?* One entirely too sure of her devotion, obviously. One who was certain he'd be forgiven. One who had met an attractive Scot ten miles back and, given the choice between her company and that of a handsome stranger, chose the latter. *Argh!*

In retrospect, she should have predicted this. After all, hadn't Jeffrey disappeared at many a ball game and party over the years? Particularly when the possibility of romance had presented itself? She whimpered low under her breath. Still, the coward should have had the nerve to tell her he was leaving, not just disappear and leave it to this couple.

"You're welcome to walk with us," the girl offered with a pitying smile that confirmed she was under the mistaken impression that Jeffrey had been Gemma's boyfriend. They were often mistaken for lovers, but aside from the fact that she'd never felt romantically interested in him, Gemma lacked something Jeffrey needed in a partner—a penis. The girl looked up at her companion. "Isn't that right, Willem?"

Red-headed, gangly and freckled, Willem nodded. "Spot on, Jenny. It's better to be with a group than off on your own," he said.

"You are going to continue, aren't you?" Jenny asked

anxiously, as though the thought had just occurred to her. "You've come so far. It'd be a shame to quit now."

That was true, Gemma knew. Still… The West Highland Way was a ninety-five mile hike that began in Milngavie and ultimately concluded at Fort William in the Scottish Highlands. Both her grandmother and mother had made the walk. It had been a rite of passage, so to speak, for the Wentworth women, who were of Scottish descent. While everyone had their own reasons for treading the path, according to her mother, Wentworth women had never failed to find clarity and peace on it, a sense of their higher purpose. They insisted that, for whatever reason, walking this trail had some sort of mystical way of putting their feet on their life's proper path.

Truthfully, Gemma didn't know if she bought into the hocus-pocus aspect of it—she was definitely dissatisfied with her life at the present—but she'd felt compelled to make the journey all the same, had felt this bizarre need to do as the Wentworth women before her. Though she would admit to feeling a strange sense of homecoming upon landing in Scotland, a loosening in her chest as it were, she was still no closer to discovering what it was that was going to make her life worthwhile, a credit to the world.

She grimaced. But she did know that her position at the bank, where she worked as a loan officer, wasn't doing it for her and if she didn't make a change soon—the right one—she was going to suffocate under her own skin.

Initially Gemma had imagined that she would have rather traveled the country in a car or luxury coach, but she had to admit she was happier making the actual walk. There was something about knowing that her feet were walking the same ground as her mother and grandmother, that they were seeing the same things—albeit generations apart—and that, while the actual journey was the same, their experiences were wholly unique. She'd met a host of interesting people, all of them of the same mind with the same ultimate goal—reaching the end of the journey—and the breathtaking views of moors and lochs were something she knew she'd never forget.

Though there were several people who were camping along the way—in designated areas, of course—most were like her, looking for an open room at a bed and breakfast or hostel. It was nothing to pass someone at one juncture of the journey and later have them pass you, sling-shotting across each other's path over and over again. That's what had happened with Willem and Jenny, which was probably why Jeffrey had entrusted them with his message and pack. The traitor, she thought again. She still couldn't believe that he'd actually left her. That he'd bailed in such a cowardly fashion, gallingly, via proxy.

They'd also been crossing paths with a beautiful, bold Scotsman she wished she hadn't noticed. Ewan MacKinnon had first caught her attention on day one from the corner of her eye and her heart had given a strange sort of jolt. Before she could get him properly in her sights, he'd vanished behind a small crowd of people, leaving her curiously dejected, as though she'd had a present snatched out of her hands. By the end of day two she'd been covertly watching for him with a keen sort of unprecedented anticipation, she'd been gratified to catch him watching her. Jeffrey's gimlet eyes hadn't missed it, either, and he had tried to get her to act on her obviously mutual interest.

An incurable romantic, Jeffrey had cited the once in a lifetime opportunity to "bag a Scottish hottie" and had reminded her entirely too helpfully about her non-existent sex life. She and her last boyfriend had parted ways eight months ago—oddly enough, she didn't like sharing and fidelity turned out to be beyond Andrew's grasp—and, despite Jeffrey's insistence that she needed a little orgasm therapy, she simply hadn't been in the mood.

Until now.

Until *him*.

She'd been having fantasies about Ewan, dreaming of him at night and daydreaming about him come the dawn. Wicked, depraved scenarios which had involved lots of heavy breathing and copious amounts of clotted cream. It was insane and yet completely undeniable. Her belly clenched, remembering, and she felt heat sizzle over the tips of her breasts. The need was secondary to the strange expectation she felt, though, this bizarre sense of destiny all tangled up with the desire.

Neither of which she had time for, especially now.

With effort, she pushed his distracting image aside and told herself to focus. She'd just been abandoned by her best friend, quite unceremoniously, on foreign soil. She grimaced.

Clearly she had bigger issues.

A quick inspection revealed that Jeffrey had left her a first-aid kit, a package of granola and quite a bit of cash. Guilt money, she thought, but it would spend just as easily and now that she'd be footing the bill for her room by herself she was going to need it.

No doubt he'd be seeing Scotland the way he'd wanted to see it to start with—in grand style, touring all the places she'd like to see as well. Rosslyn Chapel and the Royal Mile, Sterling Castle, Culloden Battlefield, Loch Ness. Though she hadn't had a chance to talk to him about it, she'd planned on asking him about changing their return tickets and spending another week in the country. It seemed a shame to leave when there was still so much she wished to do. And curiously, the idea of going back to Jackson, Mississippi—even to the quaint little farmhouse she called home—filled her with varying degrees of dread and panic.

Bizarre.

Regardless of anything, she refused to become Willem and Jenny's third wheel. Though she and Jeffrey had started on the trail early in the week, planning ahead so that the end of their walk would fall on the more congested weekend, there were still plenty of people along the way. Sticking strictly to the path, she would be safe. Or as safe as she could be, at any rate.

Perhaps this was for the best, Gemma told herself. Neither her mother nor her grandmother had taken a friend along when they'd made their walk. Maybe this was a journey she was meant to make on her own. Her gaze took in the beautiful, lush green landscape—the shaggy highland cows in the field across the street, the enormous rhododendrons—they were more like trees here than the decorative shrub variety she was used to seeing at home, the lovely thistles bobbing in the breeze—and a little sigh slipped past her lips.

Determined to think of the glass as half full, she couldn't imagine a better setting.

2

No doubt about it, Ewan decided. The animated hand-talking American guy had left her. Gemma—he'd overheard her tell someone in that lilting southern drawl. Something about her name conjured a soft warming in his chest. Caused a bizarre shift that made the balls of his feet tingle and his heart race.

Ridiculous.

He muttered a few choice expletives under his breath and passed a hand over his face. This was not his concern. *She* was not his concern. He shouldn't care that her happy-go-lucky boyfriend had abandoned her and yet...

He couldn't seem to overtake her, had purposely hung back so that he could make sure she was okay. His lips curled. Which sounded chivalrous, until one considered he'd been ogling her ass for the past six miles.

And intermittently and hungrily over the first forty they'd traversed.

There was nothing bloody noble in the way his dick had been straining against his drawers, that was for damned sure. Over a plump-reared American female whose laugh made his pulse leap.

It boggled the mind.

He'd first noticed her when they'd left Milngavie, just a fleeting glance as she blended in with the initial crowd, but there'd been something…significant, for lack of a better explanation, about that small glimpse that had stuck with him and made him purposely continue to seek her out despite the fact that she was obviously attached.

But not *too* attached, he thought, smiling. Because inasmuch as he seemed to be insanely fascinated and attracted to her, she appeared to be equally affected by him. Bad form since she clearly wasn't alone, but gratifying all the same. Hell, who didn't want to be irresistible?

Nevertheless Ewan was supposed to be taking this opportunity to figure out just exactly what it was he wanted to do with the rest of his life. This journey was supposed to be about inner reflection, getting away from the noise—the expectations of his family—and simply discover what his true path was meant be. He'd jumped around from job to job within MacKinnon Holdings, his family's business, and hadn't been even marginally satisfied with any of them. Sales, marketing, web inno-vation…they'd all left him feeling bored and unfulfilled. He needed to be *moving,* to be making a difference on a larger, global scale. To make matters worse, his father had made no bones about the fact that he was ready to retire and, as the oldest, Ewan was certain his father wanted him to step in and fill his shoes.

The mere idea made him physically ill.

Holed up in an office all day, wearing a suit and tie

to work, making decisions which would impact the family's bottom line and the ultimate income of hundreds of people, decisions that, despite having a business degree, he felt no confidence in making.

At least he was in good company, Ewan thought, because none of his younger brothers wanted to take over for their father, either. In fact, his little sister was the only one who'd ever been interested in the workings of the family company and certainly had a better grasp of it than any of the rest of them did. Surely their father would see sense soon and realize that putting Genevieve in charge would be best for all of them.

It was disconcerting that this journey was more than half through and he still didn't have a bloody clue what he wanted to do with the rest of his life. The only thing he could confidently say he wanted to do was…her. He chuckled low, pulled his water bottle from his side and took a healthy drink. Gemma trudged on ahead of him, her shapely rear making those horrid cargo pants she wore look impossibly sexy. He could tell she was tiring. She'd slowed a bit and paused every once in a while to stretch and gaze at the scenery. He wasn't fooled, of course. She needed the break.

Though he hadn't spoken a word to her, he'd be willing to bet that she'd never attempted a hike of this sort, or any other, for that matter. Her boots were new—no doubt her feet were killing her—and he'd glimpsed the top of a plain cotton tube sock when she'd paused to retie her shoe. Tube socks? Seriously? He'd thought, smiling. Newbies always underestimated the value of a good sock. He'd paid fourteen pounds for the pair he was wearing and didn't regret a single cent of it.

Self-preservation told him that he needed to avoid

her, that her misfortune didn't mean he had to be her hero. He didn't have time to be anyone's hero, reluctant or otherwise. Just because she was an inexperienced hiker alone in a foreign country didn't make her helpless. After all, she'd pressed on when her boyfriend had left, right? Definitely ballsy. But could determination, irritation and stubbornness get her up Devil's Staircase and down into Fort William? Unharmed?

Shit.

They were nearing Crianlarich and he fully expected her to find lodging there. He had planned to do the same thing, but had hoped to have enough daylight to press on to the other side of town before stopping to get a jump on the next day's hike.

He'd lagged behind her instead and now that was no longer an option. Because he'd abandoned any semblance of objectivity or good sense, Ewan knew he would "conveniently" find lodging where ever she stayed and would continue to "conveniently" mother duck her along the rest of the journey, following behind to make sure that she didn't come to any harm.

And, of course, he would stare at her ass. His lips quirked.

One had to find perks where one could, after all.

He slowed as she stopped to take another picture of another cow. How this animal could possibly look any different from the sheep and cattle they'd passed up until this point, Ewan had no idea, but she seemed determined to document every bit of wildlife between here and their final destination. It was irritating as hell and he briefly wondered if she were doing it on purpose. He didn't recall her taking so much time before. But she'd had to keep pace with Jeffrey then, and now she could move along as she saw fit.

He wasn't opposed to taking pictures—he'd snapped a few himself, particularly when they were walking the Loch Lomond stretch. Beautiful land. The mountains, hills and valleys, the taste of the loamy air. Ewan was sure the rest of the world was just lovely—and had even seen a great deal of it on various trips—but nothing could ever compare to this splendor. Cities held no appeal for him whatsoever. Too crowded, too loud, too… much. A man couldn't see the sky for all the buildings— and the smell? The combination of car fumes and concrete? No offense to urbanites, but it wasn't for him.

But then what *was* for him? He didn't have any problem figuring out what he *didn't* like; it was nailing down his preferences which seemed to be the problem. He had no idea what prevented his family from being exasperated with his continued indecision, but miraculously—sometimes irritatingly—they were all behind him, waiting patiently for him to find his true course.

Truthfully, what Ewan liked to do wouldn't be of any help to the family business. Somehow he didn't see going into war-torn countries or natural disaster–affected areas—like New Orleans after Hurricane Katrina, where he'd volunteered with the Red Cross—or any other place he was needed—just his two hands and a willingness to work—contributing to MacKinnon Holdings' bottom line. Just the opposite, really, because in seeing the need, one also saw how much capital was required to truly make a difference.

Foolishness, Ewan told himself, scowling. He needed to be figuring out what skill he could bring to the company, something profitable his father would be proud

of. MacKinnon Industries had many diversified holdings, from woolen goods to boat-making—his youngest brother's calling—and all services in between. His
father had given him a list of their interests and had told
him to look it over, to see if anything struck his fancy.
Because he'd wanted a more organic epiphany, Ewan
had avoided looking at it. He glumly suspected he'd be
perusing it soon.

While he'd anticipated that she'd stop at the first B&B
they came to, Gemma inspected the garden and moved
on. For reasons he couldn't explain, B&B number two
didn't make the cut, either. Dusk was settling and though
he had out a torch, he wasn't sure if she did. Sure enough,
she paused and began rummaging through her bag. She
set it aside and started rifling through another—Jeffrey's
no doubt—and the sound that emerged from her throat
when she didn't find what she was looking for made the
hair on the back of his neck stand on end.

It also made him grin. She had a bit of a temper, that
one. For some irrational, crack-brained reason, he liked
that.

"He took the damned flashlight!" she exclaimed to
no one in particular in a voice that brought the phrase
"last straw" immediately to mind. Another growl of
frustration. "Why would he need a flashlight? *He's* not
here. *He* left." She kicked his bag with her little booted
foot.

Ewan was so startled, he laughed aloud.

"He's sorry," she said in mocking tones, gesturing
wildly. She gave it another kick and when that didn't
satisfy her irritation, to his astonishment, in a fit of
pique she started jumping up and down on the backpack.
She continued to mutter under her breath and, though

he couldn't make out everything she was saying, the occasional word came through.

Traitor was the running theme.

Ewan sidled forward and with a flick of his finger, trained the beam on her delightfully startled face. Big green eyes rounded and a sharp inhaled gasp wheezed through her soft, pink lips. She stopped jumping at once, which was good because it made it easier to stare at her.

And stare was really all he could do.

Every muscle in his body had decided to atrophy, with the exception of the one in his chest, which was pounding harder than ever; a rush of heat swept over him, followed by an immediate cold sweat. Something happened to the air in his lungs—there seemed to be less of it—and a whirling sensation tugged behind his navel, making his stomach pitch in an expectant roll. Ewan didn't have to be a psychologist to know that he was on the brink of something—insanity, probably—yet something about this moment—this particular instance in time—was oddly more important, more singular than any other. And for reasons he couldn't explain and would sound completely irrational to any right-minded person, he knew without a shadow of a doubt, with absolute unwavering certainty, that whatever his purpose, this girl was a part of it.

His legs wobbled, startling the voice out of him.

"Any particular reason you're abusing your cargo?" he asked, his voice more normal than he would have imagined given his recent revelation, an epiphany of epic proportions.

Bloody hell. This was *so* not what he'd been looking for.

3

"GOOD GRIEF! You scared the hell out of me!" Gemma panted, clutching her hand to her chest to keep her heart from bursting through. One minute she'd been in the middle of a good old-fashioned bucket-kicking fit—or in this case, *backpack*-kicking fit—and the next, he'd startled the life out of her with his flashlight.

Her cheeks burned when she realized he'd obviously seen the whole thing. Which he would have, because he'd been following her since lunch. She'd just gotten so irritated over the fact that Jeffrey had taken the flashlight—which she knew he wasn't really going to need, since he'd gone off with his friend and was probably in a cozy hotel room by now—that she'd forgotten about Ewan being there. Truth be told, though she'd tried to embrace the whole zen approach to her friend abandoning her on this journey, the more she'd walked the more irritated she'd become. Hell, this wasn't a party or a ball game or some other social event he'd left her at—this was in the middle of a foreign country. Furthermore, the more time she'd spent in her own head the more she'd been forced to realize two things: One—other than wanting to make a profound difference of some sort, she was no closer to knowing what the hell she wanted to do with her life than she had been during the first mile. And two—if she didn't stop thinking about/ lusting after/burning for the sexy Scot who'd been trailing her since midday, there was no way in hell she was going to get any closer to what she was looking for.

Unless of course, she was looking for him…

Nonsense, Gemma thought before the idea could take hold. Leave it to Jeffrey to plant ideas in her head. This was supposed to be a spiritual experience, one with *true* meaning.

Although staring into his eyes—a warm hazel that put her in mind of sunlight through lacy cedar leaves— she could see where being with him, in any capacity, could have true meaning. Her heart gave a sudden lurch in her chest and the air thinned in her lungs, leaving her momentarily breathless and light-headed. She felt like she was floating, tethered to the earth only by his gaze and the longer she looked at him, the more the sensation strengthened. Her palms tingled and her heart vibrated faster and suddenly it was all too much.

He blinked then, thankfully severing the strange connection.

How on earth had she forgotten that he'd been behind her? Especially when she'd been keenly aware of him all day? Though she didn't have any proof, per se, she seriously suspected he'd been staring at her ass a good majority of the time. Wishful thinking? she wondered, but secretly hoped not. Truth be told she was quite vain about her ass. It was by far her best feature. Though she wasn't the president of the Itty Bitty Titty Committee, she was a card-carrying member who was especially thankful for the padded push-up bra. False advertising? Possibly, but she preferred to put her best boobs forward, as it were.

"My apologies," he said in a voice that made her insides shiver. It was slightly husky, deep and masculine. "I'd only thought to help." He gestured to the flashlight. "I take it you were looking for one of these?"

She chewed the inside of her cheek as renewed irritation rushed through her. Damned Jeffrey. She was so going to make him pay for this. "Yes, I was."

"And your boyfriend took it?"

She snorted, picked up both packs and dusted them off before putting them back on her shoulders once again. She wasn't at all herself and talking to him was only making it worse. "Jeffrey was not my boyfriend."

"He's definitely more boy than man, that one," Ewan said, an unmistakable chord of anger in his intriguing Scottish brogue. She loved the accent, the rolling lilt to it. It was so different from what she was accustomed to hearing. And the misplaced irritation on her behalf was quite nice, she thought, suppressing the urge to preen.

She started forward and he fell into step beside her, lighting their path. She felt the air crackle around them, wishing vainly that she'd gone ahead and stopped at the last B&B. Her feet were aching, she was hungry and it was getting darker and darker by the minute. She wasn't exactly certain why she'd pressed on, been so reluctant to stop, but imagined it had something to do with the long lonely evening that stretched ahead of her. She was supposed to have shared this experience with her best friend. They were supposed to have sighed over hot tea, salivated over scones, clotted cream and jam and then bitched about their respective blisters.

Instead he'd answered a cock call and she was all alone.

Her gaze slid to the imposing presence beside her and she felt a knife of heat slice through her.

Okay, she silently amended, not *all* alone.

"So he just left? The boy you were traveling with?"

Gemma released a long-suffering sigh. "He did."

Had Jeffrey really been her boyfriend, this could have been potentially as humiliating as the time she'd walked out the bathroom with her skirt tucked into the back of her pantyhose at church. The choir and pastor had gotten quite a little peep show as she'd made her way down the central aisle of the sanctuary. Thankfully, Ms. Betty Billings had come to her rescue, jerking her into the pew beside her before Gemma'd been able to go any farther. Ms. Betty had had quite a grip for someone so old and frail, Gemma remembered.

"You seem more angry than heartbroken," Ewan remarked.

"I'm extremely pissed, a bit disappointed, but not the least bit heartbroken."

"Strange," he said, giving her a good once over. She felt that perusal slither over her like a caress and had to squelch a shiver. Something hot and achy curled in her womb and she found herself lessening the distance between, curiously longing for any contact, even that of the casual variety. "You don't seem the least bit drunk to me."

She felt her eyes widen. "Drunk? I'm not drunk."

"But you said—" He sighed and shook his head, his beautiful lips curling into an endearing smile. "Sorry. When you said pissed I—"

Understanding dawned and she thanked public television for the many Britcoms she'd watched on Saturday evening TV. She chuckled. "Pissed as in angry," she explained. "And don't get me wrong, my feelings are hurt." She kicked an errant rock out of her path. "Jeffrey and I have been best friends since the fourth grade. He knew how important this trip was to me—" she shot him a glance "—both my mother and grandmother have made the walk," she explained, "and the fact that he abandoned me in a foreign country for a potential hook-up is a bit disturbing, but—"

His eyes rounded and he gave his head a little shake. "He's your best friend? A hook-up? You aren't—?"

"Together?" she finished for him. Gemma grinned. "No, not the romantic sense of the word. I'm not Jeffrey's type."

She couldn't be sure in the failing light, but she thought she saw a little bit of smugness light his smile. "Well, if he's left you for a hook-up, then he's obviously not altogether right in the upper-story."

She laughed. "He's not right on any level," she said, releasing a small sigh. "But he is dear and at some point I might even forgive him." Her eyes narrowed. "But I will make him suffer a bit first, I think."

A bark of laughter erupted from his throat. "You sound like you look forward to that."

"Of course. He deserves it."

"So beautiful women aren't his type?" he asked, once again treating her to one of those all-over glances that made her middle go all warm and gooey.

"No," she said, chewing the inside of her cheek. "In fact, women aren't his type at all."

A beat slid to three, then "Oh," he said, shooting her a significant look. "He's—"

"—gay," she finished. Coming out hadn't been a particularly easy experience for him, but he'd had the support of his friends and family and was determined not to live a lie. She admired her friend for that. It took a tremendous amount of courage to be different.

Ewan merely shrugged. "To each his own," he said, earning golden brownie points for his attitude. Any guy who'd ever been uncomfortable being around her friend went immediately on her Do Not Date list.

They walked in silence for a few moments and she simply enjoyed the kiss of the breeze on her face, the sound of music ebbing in and out of a pub farther up the street. The shop fronts were smaller here—she hadn't seen a single big box store—as were the cars and streets. Odd when one considered the vastness of the land, the sheer size of the mountains, burns and lochs. Stone houses with roses climbing their faces and spilling over the fences marched in cozy rows along the street, reminding her of Thomas Kincaid paintings. She was hammeringly aware of Ewan—he towered over her, making her feel quite dainty as he walked beside her, adjusting his longer stride to accommodate her shorter one, and a smooth woodsy fragrance accompanied his heat.

Because she'd taken every opportunity to covertly observe him for the past several days, she knew his hair was more brown than red, naturally curly and his ruddy complexion complemented his striking hazel eyes. Those eyes… They simply made her melt when she looked into them—and his smile? *Mercy.* He had a noble brow and a bold nose and a mouth that was unrepentantly sexy. Beneath it was an auburn soul patch and something about that little bit of groomed hair made him look strangely aristocratic and rebellious. She rather liked it and found herself struck with the urge to rub her thumb over it, to see if it was as soft as it looked.

Furthermore, because she was innately curious, she couldn't help but wonder what it felt like when he kissed a woman. Gemma had never cared for a mustache or a beard—too abrasive—but she suspected the soul patch would feel different…particularly against the more sensitive parts of her body. Like her nipples. They instantly pearled behind her bra and she smothered a whimper.

She'd bypassed ogling and moved directly into lust.

Not good. Particularly when one considered the way he made her feel, breathless and shaky and expectant.

"I'm Ewan MacKinnon, by the way," he told her extending his hand in a courtly gesture. "I don't think we've been formally introduced."

They hadn't, but she'd known his name because she'd overheard him say it to someone else. His hand engulfed hers and the combination of warmth, size and electricity made her fingers tingle and a tangle of sensation snake low in her belly. She felt the reaction to his touch spread through her, setting off a bizarre warning she knew she wasn't going to heed. He made her ache, made her want, made her need in a way more powerful than she'd ever experienced, as though something stronger than sexual attraction was pulling them together.

"Gemma Wentworth," she said breathlessly.

"From the States," he remarked. "The South, I would assume."

She laughed. She was used to getting the you're-not-from-around-here speech when she was visiting other areas of her own country, but having people an ocean away remark upon it was a bit surreal. "Mississippi," she confirmed. "Jackson, specifically. What about you? You're a native, right?"

"I am."

When he didn't elaborate, she didn't press. "And have you always wanted to make this walk?" Was that a B&B ahead? Gemma squinted. It definitely looked like it. Her kingdom for a scone, a hot shower and a bed.

"Not always," Ewan admitted with a chuckle. "It was more of a spur of the moment thing."

For whatever reason, she imagined that Ewan MacKinnon and spur of the moment were well-acquainted.

"It was supposed to be a journey of self-discovery," he confided, shooting her a charmingly wry smile. Her heart gave another jump in response, then a squeeze for good measure.

She inclined her head. "Ah. And what have you discovered thus far?"

He blew out a breath and grinned, then rubbed the back of his neck. "Not a whole hell of a lot, actually."

She laughed, finding both the admission and the accompanying smile ridiculously endearing. "I know what you mean," she murmured under her breath, her eyes widening significantly. Her gaze darted ahead. That was definitely a bed and breakfast. The Waterhouse, the sign said. It sounded wonderful. Beyond wonderful. Heavenly. Though she was thrilled to be walking with him and appreciated his company, she quickened her pace.

"In a hurry now, are you?" Laughter lurked in his voice.

"There's a B&B ahead and I'm beat."

"You passed two already," he remarked.

"Did I?" she asked breezily, knowing full well that she had. She cast him a sidelong glance and that bizarre sense of expectancy struck her again. She hadn't looked forward to the evening alone, but now that he was walking with her—and clearly had no intention of leaving her—her outlook had changed.

Most drastically.

In fact, she might be inclined to forgive Jeffrey more quickly than anticipated because she suspected her friend had, through his own selfish nature, done her a big favor.

And that big favor was walking right beside her.

4

HER CHEEKS PINKENED from the change in temperature, a rosier hue on her especially ripe mouth, Gemma Wentworth was even prettier in proper lighting. There was a stubbornness in the tilt of her chin, and something about her up-turned nose and the slope of her jaw, the creamy porcelain skin, was particularly adorable.

Just looking at her—and he couldn't seem to be able to *keep* from looking at her—made an odd sensation swell in his chest. Though he'd only met her, everything about her seemed strangely familiar, new but…not. His hands perpetually itched to touch her—just to feel her skin against his—and though it was counterproductive to what he was supposed to be doing on this walk, he knew that he was going to have to touch her.

A lot.

In intimate places.

Furthermore, though it sounded improbable to his own mind, he felt on a level deeper than logic and intuition that he was supposed to meet her, that their paths had crossed for a reason. He could feel that connection even now—a low thrum between them—and wondered if she sensed it as well.

With brisk efficiency the innkeeper checked them in and assigned rooms. "Dinner's over, of course, but I've got meat pies, bread and cheese."

Gemma shuddered with unabashed delight. "That sounds marvelous."

The older lady smiled kindly. "Why don't you go upstairs and wash up and I'll put a tray in the parlor for you?"

"Thank you," Gemma told her.

"Hungry, are you?" Ewan asked her as he followed her upstairs.

She shot him a look over her shoulder. "Ravenous," she admitted. "I skipped lunch and the granola I snacked on along the way isn't staying with me."

She'd likely lost her appetite at lunch, Ewan ruminated, when her friend bailed on her. Best friend or not, that was badly done. Of course, Ewan was reaping the benefits of Jeffrey's bad behavior, so he wasn't going to rake the man over the coals too much. Had her friend not left her, no doubt he'd still be watching her from a distance instead of basking in her company. Point of fact, if he ever saw Jeffrey again, he probably should thank him.

"Ah, here we are," Gemma said, slipping her key into the lock. She shot him a gratifyingly hopeful look. "See you downstairs?"

"Certainly," he said. "I'm pretty hungry myself." He could quite happily eat her up, as a matter of fact. He imagined licking a path up her inner thigh and felt his dick harden.

Damn, he was in trouble.

She smiled then, almost shyly, and then turned and ducked into her room. Ewan released a pent-up sigh and shook his head at his own stupidity. He found his own room, fortuitously located right across the hall from hers, then let himself inside. Single bed, floral wallpaper, local prints. Lacy curtains covered the windows and a door opened to the en suite bath. Though he hadn't planned on doing any checking in, he pulled his cell phone from his backpack and called Cam, his younger brother.

Predictably, he was busy—a tour bus of happy murder mystery party goers were en route to the castle and a stalking party had just left for a two-day hunt—but also predictably, Cam always had time for a chat.

"I didn't expect to hear from you," his brother said. "I take it the road of enlightenment hasn't been too illuminating?"

Ewan chuckled. "Something like that, yes."

"Keep wandering, big brother. It'll come together for you. And if what comes together for you doesn't coincide with Dad's plans, then so be it. Sometimes you have to fight for what's important."

Cam knew all about that, Ewan thought. He'd certainly bucked the status quo when he'd gone against their father's wishes and bought his estate. But Cam had always been like that—fearless, always ready for a challenge and never afraid to face life head-on.

"What makes you so sure that he doesn't think you'll come through for him?" Ewan asked. "Don't think that he has given up on the idea," he warned him.

Cam chuckled darkly. "He might as well," he said. "I know where I belong and it's here at Castle MacKinnon."

He envied him that knowledge, Ewan thought with an inward sigh.

"Alec is dead set against taking over the company as well," Cam said.

"Even if Dad let him do it from a boat?" Ewan teased. His youngest brother had an affinity for the water that bordered on the mystical. He'd been obsessed with floating things from the time he was a little kid and had studied with one of Scotland's premiere boat builders. He was happiest, they all knew, when he was on the seas, looking at a horizon. Hell, even when he came home he was taking the skiff out on the loch in front of the house within half an hour of being there. His soul would shrivel up and die if he had to take over for their father.

"Genevieve called me yesterday," Cam said. "She's losing patience. Dad told her that when one of us stepped up to do our duty he'd stop relying on her so much."

Ouch. He could see where his sister, who'd been their father's shadow since she was old enough to walk, would have a problem with that.

"For such a smart man, he's been unforgivably stupid, don't you think?" Cam remarked. "Genevieve is the obvious best choice. Why can't he see it?"

"Who knows?" Ewan said. "Mom's going to have to say something, I think."

"She doesn't want to interfere and says that it's better if Dad works it out on his own."

"But he's not working it out."

"When the three of us refuse, he'll have no other choice, right?" He hated forcing his father's hand like that because it made him feel ungrateful when, in truth, he wasn't. He just wanted to do his own thing, that was all.

Of course, his argument would be better if he actually had his own thing.

Instead of coming up with a viable job in the company, what he really wanted was to go to Haiti and help the earthquake victims. According to the article he'd recently read about the need, there were more than fifty-five thousand people still living in tents. He had no idea what he would do—what he could do even—but he was able and willing to do whatever was needed. There was honor in that purpose, a sense of satisfaction from knowing that whatever he did was going to make a difference. Was that too much to ask?

After catching up on a few more things and promising to call when he reached Fort William, Ewan disconnected. He made quick work of unpacking his bag, washed up and made the return trek back downstairs to the parlor.

He was taking his first sip of hot tea when Gemma entered the room. She'd exchanged her boots for pink bunny slippers and had taken her hair out of the ponytail she'd worn all day. Long fawn-colored curls—the exact shade of tablet candy, his favorite, naturally—tumbled over her shoulders and down her back. She'd washed her face, making her nose and cheeks shiny in the firelight. He didn't know what was more endearing, that glowing button nose, or the slippers.

"Better?" he asked, feeling unaccountably nervous. This woman did something to him, affected him on a cellular level.

She settled into the chair opposite him and selected

a meat pie from the tray. "Immensely," she said, taking a bite. She groaned with delight.

She had the sexiest mouth, Ewan noted. Full and bow-shaped, the lower lip considerably plumper than the upper. She had a bit of pastry stuck in the corner and he watched with rapt attention as her pink tongue darted out and captured the errant bit. He knew she didn't mean it as a sexy gesture, but that didn't keep his blood from heating all the same. The nagging sense of awareness that had plagued him since again setting eyes on her had quadrupled in the past hour, pushing an already irrational attraction into especially dangerous territory.

Ewan was well acquainted with sexual desire and every nuance that entailed. What he wasn't used to was wanting someone with this level of intensity. The combination of the virulent attraction and the warm, melting sensation in his chest when he looked at this particular female was, in a word, terrifying.

If this desire didn't begin to wane soon then he might just self-combust.

"Is something wrong?" she asked. "You look a little strange."

True enough, he imagined. He certainly felt strange. "I'm fine," he said, expelling a heavy breath through a grim smile. He helped himself to a piece of bread.

"So I take it you're going to continue on to Fort William?" He knew the answer, of course, but needed a conversational opener.

Chewing thoughtfully, she nodded. "Of course. Jeffrey was here for company, but my goal hasn't changed. This is a rite of passage," she said. "Both my mother and grandmother have made the walk." She frowned. "I thought I'd mentioned—"

He nodded. "You did," he said.

"I've come to a bit of a crossroads in my life," she admitted, another scowl wrinkling her brow. "One path is clearly marked and utterly unfulfilling."

That sounded eerily familiar, Ewan thought. He took a sip of tea. "And the other path?"

She smiled and let go a whooshing sigh. "That one is completely dark," she said, laughing. "In fact, I'm not even sure there's a path there. More like a goat trail."

He chuckled, sensing a kinship he hadn't expected. He knew the West Highland Way was a lot of things to a lot of different people, but what were the chances of him finding someone as interesting with the same reason as himself for making the journey? Call it coincidence or fate, he'd been right when he'd thought there was a reason for them meeting.

"What about you?" she asked. "What made you decide to take the walk?"

"I'm dealing with my own goat trail," he said. "I take it you've never been on a hike like this before?"

She smiled and leaned back fully into her chair. She crossed her legs and a slippered foot bobbed up and down, making the bunny ears flop. "Er...no, unless you count hiking from one end of the mall to the other. I've walked a lot of Civil War battlefields though, so in a way I guess that has helped. Physically, I can go a lot farther than my feet can, if that makes sense."

"New shoes?"

She winced adorably. "That was a mistake, wasn't it? My mother warned me."

He chuckled. "Look at it this way. They'll be good and broken in by the time you've finished."

She laughed, the sound soft and husky. "I'll try to remember that tomorrow night when my blisters burst."

"It's the socks," he told her. "You need merino wool."

She gasped, feigning outrage. "My father's a third-generation cotton farmer. He'd have a problem with that."

"He'd want you to be miserable?"

"No," she said, laughing. "It was a joke."

"So your father isn't a cotton farmer?"

She grinned. "Nope, he's an accountant. These miraculous socks you speak of, where can I find them?"

"I'll loan you a pair until we can find a shop that carries them."

"Much appreciated, thanks." She looked at him from beneath lowered lashes. "So why didn't you pass me today? Have you adopted me as your damsel in distress?"

He felt his mouth twitch with a grin and took another sip of tea, wishing it was something stronger. "Something like that, yes."

She winced. "While appreciated, you really don't have to do that. I can manage on my own. I'll stick to the path. Were something to happen, someone would be along soon enough to help me."

She was right and yet he knew he wouldn't leave her. For reasons which escaped him, he couldn't. Since there was no way he could confess that to her—how could he admit something he couldn't even explain?—he decided to take a different tack. He passed a hand over his face and donned what he hoped resembled an appropriately sheepish expression.

"Unless you object to making the walk with me, I'd rather us stay together. I started this journey on my own and, to be honest, it's a bit lonelier than I expected." He essayed a smile. "Evidently I don't like my own company as much as I thought I did."

She studied him a minute, a direct gaze that seemed to somehow take his measure, peer directly into his soul. "I don't object," she said, and there was an inflection in her voice that alerted him to the fact that she'd just made some sort of decision. "I started this journey with a companion and am now on my own." She peered at him from beneath a sweep of dark lashes. "Looks like we need each other, doesn't it?"

Need wasn't nearly a strong enough word.

He nodded, unable to speak.

"I should probably call it a night," she said, getting to her feet. "We've got an early morning and, if the itinerary I'm following is to be believed, that large conic mountain looming in the distance is Ben More."

"It is," he confirmed. "A bit of a steepish climb." He stood himself.

She paused. "Thanks, Ewan," she said.

"For what?"

"For making sure that I was all right. It was a nice thing to do."

"Would I lose your good opinion if I said I had ulterior motives?" he asked, sidling closer to her.

A grin turned the corners of her lips and she chuckled softly, then bent forward and pressed a kiss against his mouth. Blood boiled beneath the surface of his skin and a sensation so exquisite it stopped the breath in his lungs ricocheted through him. Every muscle in his body went rigid, then seemed to liquefy beneath her soft lips. She tasted like tea and strawberry jam and something else… something that was much more substantial.

Just as he finally came to his senses enough to deepen the kiss, she drew back and smiled, her warm eyes sparkling with delight and enough uncertainty to stroke his ego.

"I suspect our motives are the same," she said. "Goodnight, Ewan."

Yes, Ewan thought, dazed and ablaze. Yes, it was a good night.

And if he was reading her correctly—and he was relatively certain that he was—he'd make damned sure tomorrow night ended even better.

5

OH, SWEET merciful hell, Gemma thought as she wobbled shakily up the stairs to her room. That kiss…

Wow. Just wow.

She let herself into her room, then stripped down and moved immediately to the shower. Actually, knowing that she desperately needed to bathe and remove the hair from her thorny legs was the only thing that had prevented her from taking that kiss a whole helluva lot further. She was all in favor of dirty sex, but preferred to be clean while she was doing it. She adjusted the tap. Cave people must have had a keener sex drive to compensate for the odor, Gemma thought absently, otherwise she didn't see how the human race would have survived. She lathered up with her scented soap and sighed. She would have been a terrible cave woman.

But that didn't keep her from having Neanderthal fantasies about Ewan MacKinnon. Actually, the idea of dragging him into her bedroom held an infinite amount of appeal. She'd light a candle—her hat-tip to fire—and have her wicked way with him. Repeatedly.

And she knew he'd let her.

That was probably as intoxicating as the idea itself.

He wanted her and, despite his excuse about not enjoying his own company as much as he thought he would, she knew that he was every bit as enthralled with her as she was with him. And given the state of her hormones—the ones he'd kept at fever pitch for the past several days—she had every intention of letting this play out. There was more at work here than mere physical attraction—something almost destined, for lack of a better description. She'd felt it since the first instant she'd clapped eyes on him and the feeling had only intensified the longer she was in his presence—or even near his presence, for that matter.

Yes, she was supposed to be here to make some decisions about her life—what to do with it, specifically—and, other than knowing that she wanted to do something worthwhile, something that would make a difference, she was no closer to that goal than she'd been when she first started off in Milngavie. Regardless, she knew one thing she wanted to do and at the moment, that was *him*.

She could think of a thousand different reasons why she shouldn't do this—she barely knew him, for starters—but Gemma also knew she'd ignore them all. Her sex drive was strangling any reasoning or good sense and, though she knew it was fanciful thinking, there was a part of her that believed that this was supposed to happen. That she was *supposed* to be here, to meet him, specifically. That he was part of her path. Or maybe she was part of his.

Either way, there was something magical—fated even—in the way things had happened and, continual hum of sexual tension aside, she felt oddly relaxed when she was with him. As though a hidden part of her which was always wound tight...suddenly gave way. It was as frightening as it was wonderful.

And she could quite easily become addicted to the sensation.

Or more accurately, addicted to him.

How intriguing that they were both seeking the same sort of answer.

"You'd better give me a time limit or you'll never get me out of here," Gemma warned him. Here being The Green Welly in Tyndrum, a fantastic shop which featured everything from its own whiskey store to outdoor wear and all items in between. Gemma had already spied the heather jewelry and cashmere scarves. Her eyes had simultaneously glazed over and lit up.

Ewan consulted his watch. Despite the Ben More section, it had only taken them a couple of hours to reach Tyndrum, but if they were going to make Kingshouse by dark, then they really couldn't afford to linger here long.

"Twenty minutes," Ewan told her, which seemed completely fair to him.

They were there for an hour, during which she bought heather earrings, a cashmere scarf, a floppy hat, whiskey for her father, scone mix and clotted cream and jam for her mother and countless other items for various members of her family back in the States. Thankfully, rather than lug it around for the rest of the trip, she had it all conveniently shipped directly to her door.

Since she'd spent what should have been their time allotted for lunch in the store, they'd bought take-away sandwiches, crisps and Mars Bar Krispies, and picnicked in a shady little glen next to the River Orchy. The water rushed over the ancient stones, lending its own music. Various birds flitted among the branches above their heads and the scent of thistle and heather perfumed the dewy air.

He had no complaints.

The food was excellent and the company… The company kicked ass.

He'd learned a lot about his little damsel in distress this morning. She greeted the day with more enthusiasm than he was accustomed to, for starters. Ewan preferred to slide gently into the day. Gemma grabbed it by the balls and tugged it along in her wake. She liked extra sugar in her tea, was delighted over Nutella—something she'd never tried before—and occasionally hummed when she walked.

Still, there was so much more he wanted to know about her and he'd just thought of a clever way to make that happen. It was a camp game, but it would have the same effect.

"I've got an idea," he said.

She stopped chewing and her guarded gaze found his. A half-smile turned her lips. "Why does that instill my heart with a bit of panic?"

He laughed, struck anew at how easy it was to be with her, how *right* the world felt when they were breathing the same air. "I don't know, but it's completely unwarranted, I can assure you."

She relaxed once more. "Then what's this idea of yours?"

"I want you to show me five things in that backpack."

She blinked. "What?"

"You heard me. Five things from your backpack. It's an icebreaker of sorts. You can tell a lot about a person by what they carry with them on a journey such as this."

Her gaze turned speculative. "And you're going to do the same? Show me five things in yours?"

"Of course."

She nodded succinctly. "Okay, I'm game. Do I take them out or do you? Draw at random or select?"

"We'll do yours first, and I draw at random."

Gemma reached over and grabbed her bag, then opened the larger compartment. "You're probably going to pull out a pair of my underwear," she said, blushing slightly.

He hoped that he'd actually have her out of her underwear this evening. "Possibly." He reached in and withdrew the first thing that his fingers touched, a dog-eared tome of Jane Austen's *Pride and Prejudice*.

Ewan quirked a brow.

She dimpled. "I can read it over and over again and never tire of it."

Fair enough. He could do the same thing with his Louis L'Amour collection, but he kept that little tidbit to himself. Her choice was a literary classic—his was pure fun.

He reached in again and this time found a digital camera. "May I?" he asked.

She nodded and he powered on the device and flipped through her pictures. There were various snaps of her in front of Scottish landmarks, of those Highland cows she found so fascinating, blooming thistle, lots of sheep and the occasional ruin, but beyond that he found a few she'd taken somewhere else, presumably at home. "Who's this?"

She leaned forward, bringing her scent with her. Something light and flowery, like bottled sunshine and roses. Mouthwatering. Heat slithered through his loins. "Ah, that's my sister, Eloise."

"Younger?"

"Yes, by a couple of years. She's twenty-four."

So she was twenty-six then. He'd guessed as much. "And this?" he asked, when an image of an enormous Persian cat appeared on the tiny screen.

"That's my cat, Fitzwilliam. Fitz for short."

He turned to her and grinned. "That attached to Mr. Darcy, are you?"

She chewed the inside of her cheek. "He's one of my favorite Austen heroes, although I have to say that Mr. Knightley is a contender as well."

He sighed dramatically and scratched his chest. "How are real men supposed to compete?"

She chuckled. "They could begin by emulating," she said.

"Ah," he breathed knowingly. "Thanks for the tip."

"Do you want to read the book?" she asked, her eyes twinkling with humor. "Perhaps brush up on your hero tactics?"

"I thought I did an admirable job being a hero yester-day."

She chuckled again. "Had I needed rescuing it would have been heroic indeed. Since I didn't, it was merely nice."

"Nice?" he repeated. "That was all?"

"Nice is excellent," she said.

"But still not heroic?"

She gave her head a lamentable shake and bit her lip. "Sorry, no."

His gaze tangled with hers. "Then I'll just have to try harder."

"That's the spirit," she said, giving a little rah-rah gesture.

Laughing softly, he pilfered through her bag and extracted the last three items. A little sewing kit, a package of prawn-flavored crisps and a folded letter.

The letter instantly piqued his curiosity, but opening it felt a little too invasive. Gemma frowned when she saw it. "Let me have that, please," she said.

"You don't recognize it?"

"I recognize the handwriting on the outside, but don't know how it got there."

He dutifully handed it over and she quickly scanned its contents, blushing a deep red when she was finished.

"Something wrong?" he asked, concerned.

"No," she told him, her voice curiously strangled. "It's a note from Jeffrey. He must have snuck it into my bag before he left yesterday. I don't know how I missed it last night," she remarked, quickly folding it back up and stowing it in her pocket.

"I hope that he apologized at least," Ewan said, wondering very much what had put that particular shade of red in her cheeks.

"He did."

"Did he offer any excuse?"

"Mmm-hmm."

When she didn't elaborate, he held up the crisps. "You like these?" he asked skeptically.

She grimaced. "Of course not. They sound terrible.

They're proof. No one would have believed me if I'd just told them about them."

He smiled. "So you bought them?"

"Yes. As proof. I don't have a dictionary in that bag, otherwise I would give it to you."

"Oh, I understand the word," he said, laughing. "I'm just having a hard time comprehending the reason behind it." He sighed and shook his head, felt something in his chest lighten and ripple like a single pebble against a pond's surface. "You're an interesting woman, Gemma Wentworth."

"Thank you. I think."

He smiled at her, reached forward and loosened a strand of hair that had gotten stuck to her lower lip. "It's a compliment. Much better to be interesting than boring and predictable."

She smiled. "No one has ever accused me of being either of those things."

And he imagined no one ever would. She was a breath of fresh air, smart and pretty, clever and irreverent and sexy as hell. He knew that she couldn't be perfect—perfect people didn't exist and if they did he suspected they'd be boring—but she was about as perfect for him as a girl could get. Ewan stilled, jolted.

Now there was a frightening thought if there ever was one.

6

"I know you're going to want to kill me, Gemma, but you'll thank me for leaving later. I'm going to find my Scottish hottie and am confident that yours will make his move when I leave. Do everything I would do and more if you have the opportunity. See you at the airport. Always yours, Jeffrey."

SHE WAS SO ETERNALLY thankful that Ewan hadn't insisted on reading the letter, Gemma thought. Though Jeffrey had been right, it still would have been a bit embarrassing. And considering that she was going to do just what her friend had urged, she hoped he was equally successful as well.

"I don't know why you think it's weird that I'm taking these strange chips home," she said, unzipping his backpack now that it was her turn. "I guarantee that if you ever came to the South and had the opportunity to buy a package of white dirt, you'd do it."

Looking strangely distracted, Ewan blinked. "White dirt?"

"It's clay," she clarified, feeling around, trying to decide what to take out first. "People eat it. You can buy it in convenience stores next to the candy bars, chocolate roses and cigarette lighters."

His handsome face went comically blank. "You're putting me on."

She chuckled grimly. "I wish I was."

His brows winged up his forehead. "People actually purchase it? And eat it? *Dirt?*"

"It's because of some sort of vitamin deficiency." She settled on his MP3 player, curious about what sort of music he liked to listen to.

Ewan looked at her askance. "Do you eat dirt?"

She tried to power the device on, but the battery was dead. "Only on special occasions," she muttered, thwarted. She looked up at him. "What's the first song on here?"

"Otis Redding's 'Sitting On the Dock of the Bay.' You're joking right? About the dirt thing?"

"Otis, huh?" Gemma hummed under her breath. "I like Otis. And the last?"

"Flogging Molly. 'The Devil's Dance Floor.' About that dirt…"

"Nice," she said. She pilfered around a bit more, avoiding removing anything that felt like clothes because they were the least interesting. She pulled out a Swiss Army knife and grinned. "Ready for rabid badgers, eh?"

"Of course."

She felt something odd—cloth, but plush—and pulled it out. A startled laugh broke in her throat before she could swallow it. "Winnie-the-Pooh?"

Looking adorably mortified, Ewan chuckled and

passed a hand over his face. His lovely hazel eyes sparkled with embarrassment. "Er…I'd forgotten that was in there."

"You mean you really don't sleep with it at night?"

"It's my little cousin's," Ewan explained. "Henry. He put it in there so I wouldn't be lonely."

And he carried it instead of taking it out. That spoke volumes about the kind of person Ewan MacKinnon was. And the beauty in that? He didn't know it. "That was thoughtful. And heroic," she added.

"Carrying that stuffed animal is heroic?" he asked, a hint of incredulity in his voice. He gave his head a baffled shake. "Seriously? Why?"

"That you don't know makes it all the more heroic. Very Knightley-esque. Are you often lonely?"

He chuckled and popped a chip into his mouth. "No more so than anyone else I would think."

Gemma hummed under her breath, accepting his evasive answer without protest. It was nice. Easy. Being here with him, next to this river enjoying a cheap lunch. She loved the sound of the water slapping over the old stones, the buzz of various insects in the grass and the occasional low moo of the cows. The air was moist next to the river and tasted fresh and rich. It was lovely, all this untouched, unspoiled earth. She delved into his bag again, wondering what she'd find next. She pulled out a compass and quirked a brow. "Always prepared?"

"One needs to know where one is going. Direction is important." There was an underlying sentiment beneath his words, one she found herself extremely curious about.

"True." She smiled at him. "So how's that self-discovery you mentioned yesterday coming along?"

He grimaced and looked away. "It's not, I'm afraid."

"I imagine I threw a bit of a wrench into your plans. You genuinely don't have to walk with me, you know," she said. "I would be fine."

He laughed softly, then reached out and slid his thumb over her cheek. His touch sizzled through her, making her breath hitch and her toes curl. "Believe me, lass. You're a welcome distraction from my own company."

He was a welcome distraction from her own, as well. What was he doing here, really? Gemma suddenly wondered. Why had he decided to make this walk? Why now? What had put them literally on the same path? These were personal questions—ones he likely wouldn't answer—but she desperately wanted to know. It seemed imperative somehow, of utmost importance. She got the overwhelming impression that this chance meeting wasn't chance at all. Last night he'd rescued her with a flashlight, had lit her path to the B&B. Maybe she was supposed to shine a light for him, illuminate some predetermined route he should take.

Or maybe she was simply trying to attach a greater purpose to their brief relationship because she knew she was going to sleep with him.

Tonight, she hoped.

But, in all honesty, she didn't think so. She could feel something brewing between them. It was more than lust, significantly more terrifying. Walking with him today—spending time with him—had been easy and effortless, like sliding into a favorite pair of worn-out jeans. At one point she'd looked down and noticed that they'd unwittingly matched their gait, were literally walking in step with one another and the rush of attraction and emotion that had accompanied that realization had rattled her chest like a sonic boom. Her gaze slid over his face, the smooth curve of his lips, and an achy feeling settled deep within her womb. Heat slid through her veins, making her breathing shallow and her lids heavy.

He was beautiful, she realized, noting every angle and plane that comprised his visage. Broad brow, lean cheeks, a jaw chiseled straight off a Roman statue.

Feeling shaky, she removed the last item from his backpack. It was a small manila folder with MacKinnon Holdings scrawled in black ink across the front. She wouldn't open it—how could she when she'd hidden her own note?—but she did wonder at its significance.

"MacKinnon Holdings," she mused aloud. A family business? "Why do I get the impression that this has something to do with that self-discovery you were talking about?"

He sighed through a smile. "Good instincts, I would imagine."

She waited, hoping he'd elaborate.

"It's my family's business, you see. Import and export, a finger in every pie as it were."

Ah. "But you haven't found the right flavor for yourself, is that it?"

He picked up a rock and tossed it into the river. "Precisely. And it's not like I haven't tried."

"But it has to be one that makes you happy in the process, right?"

His gaze tangled with hers. "Yes. And my family wants that as well, believe me. They've been very understanding throughout all of this. My father actually wants to retire and none of us—my brothers, anyway—want any part of it." He gestured to the envelope. "My father put that list together for me so that I could look at what holdings we currently have and see if any of them strike a chord." He swallowed. "I haven't looked at it. I kept thinking that I'd figure it out on my own, that I'd have a stroke of brilliance, a flash of insight, an epiphany, a prophetic dream—hell, *anything*." He tossed another rock. "But so far...nothing. I'm going to have to look at that list soon and make up my mind, because I am not going back without a plan. And whatever it is—if it's wine-making in the south of France or sheep shearing in the Highlands—it'll be my purpose. I'll *make* it be my purpose. I'll *make* myself love it."

She paused, absorbing another character trait in her new companion—honor. Ewan MacKinnon, a Winnie-the-Pooh-carrying Scot, had honor. "Even if it doesn't fulfill you?"

His lips twisted with wry humor. "Does your job fulfill you?"

"Only as much as being a loan officer can," she said, laughing. "I've got a business and finance degree because my father thought that would be a good choice."

"You didn't want that?"

Her cheeks puffed as she exhaled heavily. "No, but he did."

He inclined his head knowingly. "So what do you plan to do? Keep working in a field you don't like?"

"No," Gemma said slowly. "I'm good at my job and it keeps a decent roof over my head, but I know it's not what I'm meant to do." She smiled up at him. "I was actually hoping to figure that out on this trip."

"Any luck with that?"

Her cheeks puffed as she exhaled mightily. "Not a

whit." She paused. "I know that I want to do something that makes a difference."

"Like what? On what scale?"

"On any scale. I did some work with the Red Cross while I was in college and that's the closest to being fulfilled as I've ever been."

He stared at her. "I've done some work with the Red Cross as well. I was in New Orleans after Katrina."

She gasped. "So was I! I spent a good deal of time in Alabama and Mississippi, too, and took a week of my vacation from the bank and went to the Gulf after the oil spill."

Another wondering smile. "I was there, too," he said. "In Orange Beach."

She felt her heartbeat quicken and her mouth went curiously dry. "I was in Gulf Shores."

"Only miles apart. It's a wonder we didn't meet then."

It was, Gemma thought, staring at him with new eyes. Clearly, like herself, Ewan MacKinnon had a heart for service. For making a difference when people were in need. That was what truly made her feel connected to the world, grounded, fulfilled.

"And yet we met here, in this place," he said, his eyes probing hers with unabashed interest.

She pulled a light shrug. "Perhaps then wasn't the time."

"Perhaps."

"We should probably be on our way," Gemma said. She stood and dusted the dirt from her behind. "Particularly if we want to make Kingshouse by nightfall."

"Don't worry," he said. "I've got my trusty torch if we don't. Is that heroic?" he teased.

She chuckled, then felt the breath whoosh out of her lungs when he bent his head to her mouth for an unexpected kiss. His lips were warm and firm and molded to hers with expert efficiency. A whirlwind of sensation—mostly of the hot, tingly variety—swept her up, sending gooseflesh over every bit of skin on her body. Her knees weakened and she sagged against him, clutching his shirt to stay upright. He tasted like soda and peppermint and the little soul patch she'd wondered about felt absolutely divine against her face. He slipped a big hand into her hair, kneading her scalp, and turned her head so that he could get better access to her mouth.

Lord, he felt wonderful. Better than anything had ever felt before or ever would after. She fit perfectly against him, as though a divine hand had carved him just for her, and she knew with every fiber of her being that, for the rest of this trip, being with him was going to be her purpose.

And there was precious little of it left. Where had the week gone? Why hadn't Jeffrey left sooner?

Breathing heavily, Ewan broke the kiss and rested his head against hers. His eyes were dark with wanting and a tender emotion she didn't recognize lurked in their churning depths. Her chest squeezed, startling a breath out of her. "Will you stay with me tonight, Gemma?" he asked, the question at once sincere, heartfelt and humble.

She nodded, more certain of that decision than any in recent memory. She smiled up at him. "It's true then," she said, feigning astonishment.

"What's true?"

"Scottish guys *are* easy."

With a roar of laughter, he laced his fingers through

hers and tugged her farther along the path. "Pathetic lot, aren't we?"

"Only if by pathetic you mean handsome and mysterious."

"We're only handsome and mysterious to foreigners. Our own people have our number."

And she grimly suspected he had hers. She was doomed, Gemma thought. And had never looked more forward to her own destruction.

7

GEMMA PRETENDED TO be taking stock of the foyer while he arranged for their room, but he saw her bite her bottom lip, a nervous little gesture he found unaccountably endearing. He hadn't discerned anything the least bit skittish about her over the past day and half. If she thought it, she spoke it. Or at least she did with him. She'd jokingly told him today that something about him disabled her brain-to-mouth filter.

He rather liked that.

Diplomacy had its place, for sure, but in a true relationship there should be open dialogue. Every filter should be turned off, every safeguard which had been put in place should come down. Honest communication, that was the key. But before he'd met Gemma Wentworth, he'd never been that honest and open with any woman. He'd been guarded, hesitant…respectful and charming, of course, but he'd never had the desire to be anything more than that.

Until now.

How could Fate—if that was what had brought them together—have put someone so perfect, so thrilling and so wonderful into his path only to snatch her away when this walk was over? Where had the time gone? After tomorrow night, their journey was finished. Gemma would return to her home in the States, back to her loan officer position and he'd likely never see her again.

In no way was that fair.

They'd found something special together—something rare—and it frustrated him that they wouldn't be able to explore it further. To think that they'd been only miles apart last year, that they might have even walked the same stretch of beach or eaten at the same restaurant. Who knew how many times their paths had intersected but never truly crossed? Who knew where this might have eventually led, given more time. How he would have loved to see where the rest of their walk, beyond this one, might have taken them.

Right now, thankfully—at last—it was taking them to bed.

He'd been patient, or as patient as he could be given the fact that he'd been fighting the Battle of the Great Erection all day long and losing spectacularly.

He just couldn't stop *looking* at her.

Honestly, from the first moment he'd clapped eyes on her it was as though he couldn't avoid staring at her. If she was within eyesight, then his gaze was on her. He loved the way the light turned her butterscotch curls all golden, the way the wind would tug at the curly strands playing about her neck. The smooth slope of her cheek begged for his hand and the sleek line of her brow made something in his chest clench.

He loved watching her mouth when she spoke, the shadows her eyelashes made against her lids, even her tiny little nose engendered bizarre feelings in him. There wasn't a bit of her he hadn't noticed, hadn't absorbed and, though he'd held her hand and stolen the errant kiss along the way—a mere skirmish in the Battle of the Great Erection—nothing had fully satisfied him.

Bedding her had to, otherwise he was in serious danger of losing his mind.

"Nervous?" he asked as he led her upstairs.

"Yes," she admitted.

"About what specifically? Are you afraid you won't meet my expectations?" Ewan joked. He turned the key in the lock and let them into their room. More lacy curtains, more floral wallpaper. Another room, another house. But this one would be different if for no other reason than they would share it.

She laughed softly and shook her head. "I wasn't, so thanks."

Ewan chuckled. He backed her up against the door and pressed a kiss under her jaw. "If you're not worried about satisfying my voracious sexual appetite, then what exactly is going on in that little head of yours that concerns you?"

She hummed a sigh of pleasure. "Trite as it may sound, I've…never done this before. I don't make a habit of sleeping with strangers."

He nuzzled her cheek with his nose. "Tell me honestly, do I feel like a stranger to you? Because it feels to me like I've known you forever."

She slid her hands up over his chest. "No, you don't feel like a stranger at all. You feel good," she said, sighing through her smile.

"I bet I'd feel better naked."

A sharp burst of laughter echoed up her throat. "P-probably so, but *I'd* feel better clean."

"Say no more," Ewan told her matter-of-factly, swooping her up into his arms. She gave a startled squeak, then chuckled softly. "I have a solution."

"I'll just bet you do."

He strode toward the bathroom. "We'll shower together. It's called multi-tasking. Maybe you've heard of it?"

Her ripe lips twitched with humor. "It sounds vaguely familiar."

"Any objections?"

She grabbed the hem of his shirt and tugged it over his head. "Only one. Move faster."

HE WAS RIGHT. Multi-tasking was a wonderful thing.

Staring at her as though she were the last treat on the dessert tray, Ewan reached purposefully into the shower and turned on the tap.

Then he sidled forward, bare chest gleaming, all tawny masculine hair and bronze skin, and melded his mouth to hers. This kiss was different. It was determined and desperate and had a strange sort of autocratic authority about it that, quite curiously, made it all the more thrilling. She toed off her shoes, felt his hands at her waist, then sliding over her bare hips as he eased the fabric down.

A decided bulge nudged impatiently against her belly, making her mouth water and her breathing go shallow. A low steady hum of arousal streamed through her body and concentrated in her womb. Her thighs gave a little quake as he fed at her mouth, then his hands cupped her bare bottom and gave a possessive little squeeze.

"I love your ass," he said between their joined mouths.

She reached around and grabbed his. "I love yours.

I often wished you'd walk in front of me so that I could look at it."

He chuckled low, then pulled her shirt over her head. "Why do you think I walked behind you?" His gaze lingered over her bare breasts. "No bra?"

She gave a deprecating laugh. "No need."

He thumbed a nipple, then bent and touched the tip of his tongue as it pearled in response. His mouth worshiped her breasts, teasing the tautened buds, suckling deeply, lavishing attention on each. Every lave of his tongue sent a corresponding tug low in her belly, as though an invisible cord connected the two. He let out a shaky breath, then kissed her breasts once more. "I am a very lucky man."

It was unbelievable the power that achingly heart-felt statement had immediately upon her. Her heart lightened to the point that she was surprised she didn't levitate and any reservation, however small, was suddenly burned away by the absolute certainty that she would not regret this later. A flash of heat followed by a line of gooseflesh scuttled down her spine. She stepped into the shower and tugged him with her.

He set a condom determinedly onto the small ledge in the shower, then turned to her.

Hot water, hot man...

Heaven.

He lathered a cloth and slid it over her body, testing each part for cleanliness after he'd rinsed her off. In the spirit of multi-tasking, Gemma did the same thing. She loved how his wet skin tasted against her mouth. Smooth and sleek, he was perfectly proportioned, a work of art made of muscle and bone. His curly hair turned a darker red when it was wet and his sinfully carnal mouth seemed to be everywhere on her body. Along her neck, feeding at her breasts, the backs of her knees, the soft spot between her legs.

He left no part untasted.

He was very thorough.

Legs quaking, Gemma took him in hand and worked the slippery skin, the velvety tip. He was hot and hard against her palm, making her inwardly preen with power. She was doing this to him, was making him need her, want her, as much as she needed him. Ewan was a tall, broad man and the part of him she currently enjoyed was definitely built to scale.

Mouthwateringly so.

She bent, but he stopped her with a determined touch. "No, lass. I can't wait," he said, his voice rough. "I need you too much."

She smiled and looked at him through heavy lids. "Then take me."

Eyes blazing, he made quick work of the condom, then turned her around and lifted her leg so that it rested against the ledge of the shower. A second later she could feel him at her entrance. Hot, hard and wonderful, it was all she could do not to lean back and impale herself on him.

"Please," she said. She knew he was holding back, that he was afraid he would hurt her. But this ache, this desperate need was much, much worse.

With a primal groan that made her feel thoroughly feminine, Ewan pushed into her, stretching her to the limit he filled her so completely. She inhaled sharply, savoring the exquisitely perfect feel of him inside of her. She sagged against him with relief, as though from the very moment she'd seen him this had been what she'd been waiting for.

And until this second, she hadn't realized just how true that was.

Then he began to move inside her—long, deep strokes that systematically removed thought and replaced it with sensation. She bit her bottom lip and tightened her feminine muscles around him, holding him to her. He made another one of those masculine noises—part groan, part growl—that made her feel powerful and wanted and a pulse began to quicken in her womb.

She made a few noises of her own as his tempo increased—in and out, harder and harder, his large hands anchored on her hips. She felt him shift, then the absence of water, and realized that he'd snagged the extending massaging shower head from the wall. He brought it around and nestled the hot, pulsating spray against her clit, then pushed hard and angled deep from behind. The combination of sensation—hot hard male at her back, rhythmic warm water massaging at her front.

The perfect recipe for orgasm.

She came.

Hard.

BURIED BETWEEN HER THIGHS, her sweet, beautiful ass snuggled up against him, her smooth, silky skin underneath his hands, was as close to heaven on earth as Ewan had ever been.

Then she came for him, her tight heat clamping around him, and Ewan experienced the most powerful release he'd ever had. He gritted his teeth, leaned his head back and roared.

Harder, faster, then faster still.

His balls slapped against her as he buried himself repeatedly in the softest place he knew he'd ever have the pleasure to land.

Every muscle in his body went rigid and he pounded into her with all the strength he could muster, milking the sensation for all he was worth. It drained him, exhilarated him, left him feeling weak, yet strangely energized. His heart beat a wild tattoo against his chest and his vision blackened around the edges. He lowered the shower head away from her and then, rattled to the soles of his feet, he bent forward and kissed the curve of her shoulder.

One thing became imminently clear in that moment—against reason, logic and any similarity to common sense: Gemma Wentworth was his.

She was his purpose. *She* was what he'd been looking for all along.

8

AFTER HAVING wonderful shower sex, where her emotional tears were disguised by the water, then later more enthusiastic bed sex—the springs were embarrassingly creaky—they'd gotten off to a later start than expected, but Gemma had no complaints. In fact, she was happier and more content than she'd ever been in her life. She desperately wished she could confide in Jeffrey, but calls to his cell phone went straight to voicemail.

Clearly he was busy.

At any rate, in order to make up some of the time they picked up the pace to Kinlochleven, which was made easier by the fact that it was a descent rather than a climb, and stopped there for a brief lunch.

Though they were only fourteen miles from their final destination, Gemma was finding it increasingly hard to be happy about it. There was no joy in the accomplishment because she knew she and Ewan would part ways.

She wasn't ready, and the mere idea of it filled her with a panic that all but made her vomit.

This was not at all what she'd been expecting and

imagined. Sex with Ewan—though it definitely was a spiritual experience—was not the sort of experience her mother and grandmother had had in mind for her when she'd left for Scotland. The thought made her grin. Her mother would want her to guard her heart, but she suspected she'd get a wink and a nod of approval from her grandmother.

Ewan, who'd seemingly been lost in his own thoughts, tossed his napkin onto his plate. "So I guess you'll be flying home soon?"

"Noon tomorrow," she said and if she sounded glum it was because she was. Somehow staying on, knowing that they wouldn't be together, no longer held the same appeal. Were she to see Rosslyn Chapel and all those other places she'd thought about, she'd like to do it with the man seated across from her. But he had his own things to figure out. "I've got to arrange transport back to Glasgow." She grimaced. "Jeffrey was supposed to have taken care of that." No doubt he'd meet her there. It seemed like ages ago since she'd seen her friend, but it had only been three days. How was that possible, when she felt so different?

His woefully familiar gaze caught and held hers, a wealth of unspoken things reflected there. "I'll take you, if you'd like," he said.

Bliss and agony, but she'd like nothing better if it meant they'd be together a little longer. "I'd hate for you to go out of your way."

It suddenly occurred to her that she didn't even know where he lived, what part of the country he called home. How odd, when she knew so many other things. The exact shade of his eyes, the fluted perfection of his spine, the way his soul patch felt against her belly. He was noble and clever and in possession of one of the wickedest senses of humor she'd ever had the pleasure of encountering. He made her feel special and she liked herself when she was with him. He was easy company, this gorgeous Scot, and she'd miss him when she went home.

"I would drive you to the ends of the earth were it your wish, Gemma, and it would never be out of my way, nor the slightest bit of an inconvenience."

She flushed with pleasure. Now that was very Knightley-esque indeed. "Where is home, then?" she asked lightly, hoping that he'd confide a little in her.

"Glen Kerr. It's on Loch Lomond."

She leaned forward and smiled. "A castle?"

He laughed, the sound familiar and low. "More of a manor house, I would say. I've got two brothers and a sister, so we needed a lot of room. My grandparents bought the place when they first married, but only ever had my father. He said the house was too big not to fill it with children—" he shrugged, smiled "—so they did. They live in the carriage house on the property. Only my sister and myself still live in the house. We like being close. When my sister marries, I'll move out and renovate one of the other houses on the estate."

A tiny part of her had entertained the fanciful notion of him showing up on her doorstep, but it died a very swift death in light of this new information. She'd known he had family—the company was a clue after all—but still…

"So where do your brothers live?"

"Alec is a boat builder and has a place in Lochawe. Cam has his own place, too. He hosts murder mystery parties in what he calls a 'rotting pile' up in the

Highlands. It's actually not a pile at all, but that's Cam."
He chuckled.

Gemma grinned. "It sounds fun. And you and your
sister in the house and your parents on the grounds,"
she said, releasing a little sigh. "Never lonely, eh?"

He leaned back in his chair and laughed again, a fond
smile on his handsome face. "Definitely never lonely.
No privacy, either, but…it's home," he said, meeting her
gaze, and whether he meant it to be a significant gesture
or not, it was. "What about you?" he asked. "Where
exactly is it that you live again?"

"Jackson, Mississippi. It's the capital of my state, so
it's not a small town, but I live on the fringe, as it were,
so it sort of feels like it."

"And your family?"

"Just me and my sister," she said. She envied him his
big family. Her own had never been, just an odd uncle
or two and a sprinkling of cousins she wasn't close to.

"Does she live nearby?"

She exhaled slowly. "Sadly, no. She met a guy from
New Zealand while in college and moved there last
year. They're in Auckland." She missed her terribly,
of course, but could hardly blame her for leaving. "My
parents are both retired and do a lot of mission work.
They're in Honduras right now, helping with an orphan-
age there."

He nodded. "How long have they been there?"

"This time? Three months."

His shrewd gaze studied her. "That's a long time to
be away from home."

Gemma shrugged, taking a sip of her drink. "They've
waited their whole lives to do this. I don't think it both-
ers them."

"It's admirable work, that's for sure."

It was and she could hardly fault them for doing it when she'd like nothing more than to do something similar. They wanted to make a difference and were definitely making the lives of those orphan children better. The difference between her and them was they had the money to go and do those things and…she didn't. It took cash to pay for airfare and living expenses, to be away from work for extended periods of time. She made a decent salary at the bank, and she'd socked a little back in savings, but it was certainly not enough to bankroll an extended trip into Haiti or China, two areas she wished she could offer her services, however small. Perhaps she could get into the fundraising aspect instead though, Gemma thought.

The idea budded and bloomed inside her. *That* was definitely something she could do and was in the scope of her resources. Was it the work she desperately wanted to do? Not precisely…but the end result would be the same. She'd be making a difference. She'd have a cause, a purpose, a life plan.

"That smile looks promising," Ewan said. "Dare I ask what put it on your face?"

"I just had my moment," she said. "My spiritual experience."

"I thought you'd been having those with me since last night."

She chuckled, warmth and happiness swirling through her. A goal, at last. Not the ideal one, but one that would work. It would soothe her soul.

And speaking of spiritual experiences…

Her gaze slid to Ewan. If he was driving her to Glasgow, then he'd undoubtedly spend the night with her.

That was something to look forward to at least, she thought, heartened as a delicious shiver worked its way through her. Images from last night's sex-a-thon flitted rapidfire through her brain—naked skin, smooth muscle, his big hands shaping her body, that talented mouth suckling at her breast....

He hadn't just made love to her—he'd worshiped her. Thoroughly. Sampled every part, touched every inch, paid homage to her entire being.

She pressed her knees together as warmth pooled at her center. Her clit tingled and her breasts grew heavy with want. Honestly, just thinking about him almost brought her to climax. Right now, sitting in this crowded little café, if he so much as touched her, she'd come.

Deciding a bathroom visit was in order, Gemma stood abruptly. "I'd better take care of necessary business—" she almost choked on a hysterical laugh "—before we head out."

He gave her an odd look, obviously wondering what the hell had come over her. "Of course."

IT TOOK HIM SEVEN seconds to discern that last look on her face before she left the table and he nearly sent his chair to the floor as he bolted up after her. It had been a puzzling expression—a bizarre combination of sleepy and desperate—and he couldn't believe he'd been so thick as not to recognize it, particularly after last night, when he'd seen it repeatedly.

When he'd been inside of her.

She was just opening the ladies' rest room door when he rounded the corner. "Gemma."

Her startled gaze swung to his.

He closed the distance between them, grabbed her

hand, then backed her into the room and determinedly locked the door. She didn't hesitate, but literally threw herself at him, twining her arms around his neck, aligning her sweet little body against his.

He kissed her long and deep, tangling his tongue around hers, a heady game of seek and retreat that mimicked a more intimate action he had every intention of performing. Using one hand, he awkwardly rifled through his back pocket until he found a condom, then lowered his zipper, freed his dick and slid the protection into place. She fumbled with the buttons on her pants, then shimmied them down to her ankles. Ewan stepped over them and lifted her off her feet.

"I've got…an itch," she panted between their joined mouths.

In one fluid motion he thrust up into her, seating her firmly on his cock. Like a tumbler in a lock, something deep inside of him opened up and settled into place. His chest expanded to the point he thought his lungs would explode.

"Don't worry," he grunted as he pistoned in and out of her. "I'm going to scratch it."

And he did.

9

ACHING AND EXHAUSTED, but sated and satisfied, Gemma was smiling when they finally arrived in Fort William. Ninety-five miles, on foot, and she—a delicate southern belle—had done it.

Boo-ya!

"You're quite proud of yourself, aren't you?" Ewan asked her, a smile on his lips.

She preened a bit. "Yes," she admitted. "Yes, I am."

He twined his fingers through hers and gave them a squeeze. "And you have every reason to be, lass. You're a remarkable woman."

Appreciating the compliment, Gemma let it settle into her heart and take root.

She paused and turned to look at him. "Thank you, Ewan. That means a lot to me, because I happen to think you're a remarkable man."

"I feel like one when I'm with you," he said—more of that candor that she wasn't accustomed to but sincerely appreciated.

And he *was* remarkable, Gemma realized. He was smart and kind, honorable and funny. He made her feel cherished and special and just mysterious enough to hold his attention. He made her feel beautiful and sexy and, God help her, *loved* even though she knew that was irrational. Who falls in love in three days? How could you possibly know someone well enough to fall in love in three days?

But if this wasn't love, then she didn't know what was.

Just knowing that she was going to board a plane in less than twenty-four hours made her sick to her stomach with despair.

She didn't want to leave him. She wanted to tour his country with him, hear him laugh, feel his big hand in hers as they strolled among the heather. She wanted to lie down beside him at night, put her cold toes against his legs for warmth and feel him wince, then wake up with him in the morning, her cheek against his chest. She wanted to have fights and make up, enjoy candlelit dinners and making love in front of a fire. She wanted to listen to him, not only because she loved the accent, but because every word that came out of his mouth was important to her.

Gemma thought about all of these things while he arranged for a rental and was still lost in her own head when they got into the car. Then something occurred to her and she cursed her own selfishness.

"Did you ever look at that list your brother gave you?" she asked.

Ewan gave his head a small shake. "I did not." He shot her a smile. "I've been a little distracted."

"I'm sorry," she said, meaning it. He'd had a purpose for his journey and, while she knew he didn't regret meeting her, he hadn't achieved his goal. She had, at least in as much as she was going to right now, and that felt unfair.

"Don't be," he told her, reaching over and casually lacing his fingers with hers. "I wouldn't change a thing."

"Would you like me to get the list out of your backpack? I could read it aloud to you while you drive. Maybe offer a different perspective."

He laughed softly. "Thanks, lass, but there's no need. I know what I want to do, but I just don't see how to make it beneficial to MacKinnon Industries."

"You can do anything you set your mind to," she told him.

He turned to look at her then, an unreadable expression on his face. "You really believe that, don't you?"

"Unequivocally." She swallowed, and offered a smile to lighten the moment. "What do you want to do, Ewan MacKinnon?"

He blew out a long, steady breath. "I want to make a difference," he said simply. "I want to travel the world, go where I'm needed and do the most good that I can."

Just like her, Gemma realized.

But the difference was…he could afford to do it.

"Ewan, can I ask you something personal?"

"Sure," he said without the slightest hesitation.

"I'm assuming that, given what I imagine is the scale of MacKinnon Holdings, that your family is relatively comfortable?" There, she thought. That was as tactful as she was going to be able to be.

He shot her a glance. "We are," he said. "My grandfather made good investments, so we all got a portion of his estate and my father has been quite successful."

"Is a philanthropy program already in place?"

"No," he said slowly. "Not an official program. We do some things, but…there's no system in place."

"Would that be something your father would be interested in having? Because if so, it would be the perfect job for you. You'd be serving a purpose in the company and making a difference."

She didn't have to see the wheels turning in his head to know that they were. A big smile broke out over his face—one very similar to the one she'd had after lunch earlier—and he abruptly pulled the car over and kissed her soundly.

"All-righty, then," she said when she could breathe again. "What was that for?"

"For being brilliant," he said. "That's the perfect solution. The infrastructure is in place, we have the capital to truly do it properly and we have me, the eternal wanderer who can go wherever I'm needed, wherever I can make a difference. Bloody brilliant!" he said again, staring at her with so much joy she could feel it as well. "Thank you, Gemma," he said, his voice rife with heartfelt meaning. He pulled back onto the road once more. "You just changed my life."

Quid pro quo, she thought. He'd certainly changed hers.

"What about you?" he asked suddenly. "Your spiritual experience that didn't have anything to do with my masterful lovemaking skills? What are you going to do with the rest of your life?"

"I'm going to do the same thing you are," she said. "Only from the fundraising aspect of it."

Just then a large gray stone house came into view, a loch off to the side and a forest all around. She frowned.

She'd thought they'd stay in a hotel in Glasgow, but this was obviously a private residence.

His, she realized. She swallowed tightly.

It was stately and beautiful with a huge front door and a pebbled drive. She fell instantly in love with it. "Where are we?" she asked, her heart rate quickening in her chest.

"My house," Ewan confirmed. "I thought we could spend the night here."

She got it now, Gemma thought, as he pulled up in front of the house. She could completely see why this was home, why he hadn't left.

If this were her home, she'd never want to leave it, either.

But she'd have to, and she'd be leaving him in the process. A yoke of sadness settled around her heart and tugged at her shoulders with its weight; every fiber in her being fought against that impending departure. The moment when she'd have to tell this magnificent man goodbye.

"YOU CHARMED MY FAMILY last night, you know," Ewan said as he helped her out of his SUV. Despite his driving slow enough to anger other drivers, they'd finally made it to the airport. He knew that Gemma was dead on her feet. Because he was a selfish bastard, he'd kept her up all night, alternately talking to her and making love. But he couldn't seem to help himself. With every tick of the clock, he could feel their time together drawing to a close and he didn't want to waste a single minute of it by doing something as trivial as sleeping.

"You have a great family," Gemma said. "I hate that I didn't get to meet Alec or Cam."

"Not as much as they'll hate not getting to meet you," Ewan told her, grinning. "You'll be hot gossip for weeks on end." People rushed past them, dragging wheeled baggage, burdened with carry-on items. From the corner of his eye he saw her friend Jeffrey standing near the ticket counter, talking with a man in low tones. Jeffrey didn't look particularly happy.

She laughed. "Why is that?"

"Because I've never brought a woman home with me before. You're special, Gemma. More special than you realize."

He watched the muscles move in her delicate throat as she swallowed. "So are you, Ewan. I can't tell you how much I appreciate you making the last bit of that walk with me. I have enjoyed every minute that we've—" Her voice wavered and he watched as her eyes grew damp with tears. "I'm no good at goodbyes," she finally managed, dashing a tear away.

Evidently he was more selfish than he'd ever counted on because he suddenly found himself incapable of letting her leave. He'd told himself that he wouldn't do this. That he wouldn't ask her to give up her home for his. But that was exactly what he intended to do. And if she wouldn't stay, then he would follow her.

"Then don't say goodbye," Ewan said, framing her face with his hands. He dropped his forehead to hers. "Don't go," he implored her. "I know that you have a home and a family and a country all your own…but I don't want you to leave. Stay with me, Gemma. Make a life with me. Here. And if you can't do that, then take me with you. Because I am yours. Utterly and completely, hopelessly yours."

"You'd do that for me?" she asked breathlessly. "You'd leave here?"

"In a heartbeat." And he knew it was true. Scotland was his homeland, for sure, but home was wherever Gemma was. They could travel the world *together*, make a difference *together*.

A slow, wondering smile slid across her ripe lips and she laughed aloud. "Are we crazy?"

"Definitely," he said, sliding a finger along her jaw. "But I don't see how that signifies."

She looked up at him, her green eyes tangling with his. "I'll stay with you," she said, and he'd never heard four more beautiful words. His irrational heart burst with happiness and he bent his head and kissed her upturned mouth.

The next walk they'd take would be down the aisle.

THE WARRIOR

1

SUMMER DAVIES TOOK one look in the mirror at her reflection, gasped in horror, then met her mother and aunt's gaze over her shoulder. *"Oh, hell no."*

Their similar faces fell. "Oh, come now, Summer, it's not as bad as all that," her aunt Mimi told her. "So you're coming out of the top of it a little. If you've got it, flaunt it, that was always my motto," she declared as she adjusted her own cleavage and Summer knew she meant it. Lamentably, Aunt Mimi didn't let *not* having it stop her flaunting it and watching her aunt arrange her breasts was a little more than Summer cared to see. "You look lovely, dear. Trust me."

And yet she didn't.

Summer groaned and studied the dress with mounting dread. She looked like an eighteenth-century prostitute and an exceedingly impoverished one at that, otherwise she would have more fabric on her costume. She made another futile attempt at cramming her breasts down beneath the bodice. Granted, she didn't know a whole lot about the proper attire for this time period, but she'd read enough Regency romance novels to know that this was off. Wasn't she supposed to have a shawl? A fichu? Hell, at this point she'd settle for a doily and made a mental note to snatch one off a table when they returned to the library.

A murder mystery party, she thought with a mental eye roll. Her? She'd never taken any drama classes and regardless of how many clues she was supposed to drop or the nuggets of insight that were aimed her way, she knew she was going to be utterly terrible at it. Thankfully she'd had the forethought to check the little-to-no-involvement box, meaning she hoped that they'd heed her wishes and limit her role. Point of fact, dying off early would be a treat.

But ultimately what did it matter what she thought? This entire trip to Scotland wasn't for her—it was for her mother and her aunt—and she was merely there to prevent them from getting into too much trouble. Left to their own devices who knew what the two widowed sisters would do? They were certainly notorious in Little Cabbage Valley, Kentucky. Her aunt owned the local dramatic theater—and starred in every production, of course—and, in addition to her regrettable addiction to bubble wrap, was a little too fond of her sipping whiskey. She hoped her aunt got a starring role, Summer thought. She'd eat up the attention.

As for her mother… Summer watched her mother slide her hands over the pretty hunter-green gown she'd been given to wear for this first night of the murder mystery party.

Her mother was what everyone lovingly called a character. With a sharp wit and a kind tongue, she was brilliant, tenacious, opinionated and a bit loud—and since her husband had passed away, she'd been a shell of her former vivacious self. Summer had always thought of her mother as a pillar of strength and seeing her brought so low had been almost as horrible as her father's death. It was heartbreaking as she watched a little more of the life fade from her mother's eyes every day.

That was why she was here, she reminded herself. That's why she'd play *Court In the Act*—she heaved an internal sigh—a murder mystery set in Regency England, among Prinny's intimate set. His mistresses, to be precise, and from the looks of her gown, she was one of them.

To make matters worse for her mother, the day after her father's funeral, Moose, their chocolate Lab had had a seizure and died. Losing Dad and then the beloved pet they'd had for ten years had almost sent her mother over the edge. When she'd found her mother curled up asleep in the dog bed, using her father's bathrobe for a blanket, Summer had been seriously afraid for her mental health.

That's why she'd ultimately agreed to make this trip with her.

Her parents had been planning this vacation for years, saving their money, poring over brochures from the travel agency. They'd pieced together an itinerary, mapped everything out and had finally saved enough cash to do everything they wanted to do without having to take their dream trip on a shoestring budget.

And then, quite unexpectedly, he'd died.

Winston Davies had been a fit fifty with no history of heart disease when the attack had hit. One minute they'd been planting tulip bulbs, the next…he was gone. And the world as they'd known it had changed forever.

Ultimately, it was Aunt Mimi's idea not to cancel the

trip, which had been booked months before her father's passing. Mimi had insisted that her mother needed the vacation and frankly, though it felt weird turning her parents' intended romantic getaway into a girl-bonding mission, Summer couldn't agree more. Her mother had brought along some of her father's ashes and was sprinkling them in all the places they'd planned to visit. She'd insisted that she could feel him with her and who was Summer to argue. Other than the visible strain and the melancholy sadness around her eyes, what did Summer *truly* know of her mother's grief?

Dealing with her own was hard enough.

"Charlotte Ann, that dark green looks fabulous on you," Mimi told her sister. "I'm so glad that we're doing this," she enthused, smoothing a wrinkle out of her own outrageous gown. "A *real* murder mystery party in a *real* Scottish castle." Mimi turned to Summer and arched a droll brow. "Honestly, you can't tell me you don't find this a little exciting, Summer."

Oh, yes she could, but she wouldn't. She'd leave the drama to the two of them, thank you very much. It exhausted her.

Truthfully, she found the castle and grounds quite fascinating. She liked the feel of it, the very air, if that made sense. She'd taken a deep breath when they'd gotten off the bus, absorbing the atmosphere around the place, and something about that long inhalation had satisfied her better than any breath she'd taken before. It had been strange but wonderful and had a fated-ness about it she couldn't explain.

Though she'd been in love with the country since she'd seen her first pink-painted sheep and had thoroughly enjoyed every minute of the Royal Mile and the various castles they'd visited, this one had completely enchanted her. The house and the grounds were stately, but imperfect—the tapestries that lined the walls were a bit faded and frayed and the floors were scarred from centuries of use—but it was those things that made it feel more like a home and less like a museum. The owner, one gorgeous Scot named Cam MacKinnon, actually lived here, in the house. She flushed, remembering him, and an odd rush of warmth flooded her veins.

He was easily six and half feet tall, broad shoulders with a healthy ruddy complexion and a pair of bright blue eyes that were the exact shade of the Morning Glories that climbed her porch railing at home. The shade was startling enough on its own, but paired with that dark, curly, auburn hair it was particularly striking. He had a wide, full mouth and a long dimple in his right cheek when he smiled that she found oddly endearing. He had a commanding presence, as though he was used to leading—to fighting for what mattered—and she could easily see him on the cover of one of her Scottish historical romance novels aside a horse with a gleaming claymore in hand.

Though she was used to seeing a masculine form or handsome face and noting them with pleasure—she was a healthy young woman after all—she wasn't used to the purely visceral reaction she had to *this one*.

She'd taken one look into those amazing eyes and completely forgotten herself. He'd merely introduced himself, reached out and clasped her hand and she'd become a quivering pile of goo on the spot. She'd felt the stupid smile sliding over her face before she could stop it, but honestly had been more concerned over the sudden dampness in her panties and instantly erect nipples to seriously worry over the smile. To her horror and embarrassment, he'd noticed the nipples—she'd been wearing a thin T-shirt at the time—and she briefly wondered if he'd chosen this costume for her himself to taunt her with the reminder of her own cleavage. The irreverent twinkle she'd noticed in his eyes when she'd first met him certainly lent truth to her supposition.

At any rate, they'd gotten their parts, costumes and accessories for this farce and were due in the library for drinks momentarily. She'd read her character booklet, noted which secrets she was supposed to tell which characters and was ready to bribe, borrow and steal her way out of the game.

"I wonder when we'll get our weapons?" her aunt Mimi asked. "I hope I get something good. Like poison or a dagger."

Who knew her aunt was so ghoulish?

"I wonder if Mr. MacKinnon will be playing Prinny himself."

"He'd need to gain a few pounds to make it believable," Mimi said. "Did you see him, Charlotte Ann? Mercy, his arms were like boulders."

Her mother grinned. "I hadn't noticed."

Mimi turned to her. "You noticed, didn't you, Summer? He's definitely leading man material."

"As our host, I don't think he'll actually be playing."

Mimi's face fell. "More's the pity." She turned back to her mother and immediately started strategizing. Watching her mother and aunt giggle like school girls and plan their game, Summer smothered a sigh and pasted a happy look on her face. If her mother was happy, she had no choice but to be as well.

"Shall we go down?"

"Let's do," Mimi said. "I could use a drink."

Summer shared a significant look with her mother, one that Mimi didn't miss. She scowled, her brows lifting in a haughty arch. "I know to keep my wits about me," she admonished. "I'm not a child, for pity's sake."

Maybe not, but they'd had to help her remove her shoes last night because "the floor kept moving on her." Making sure that her aunt had a stash of bubble wrap stowed away in her little sachet, the three of them set off.

"I hope it's none of us who get killed," her mother said. "Wouldn't that be just terrible?" she tsked.

Humph. Summer hoped she got killed off first. Hell, she'd volunteer. Maybe if she got murdered early, she could take her camera down by the loch. She'd framed half a dozen shots in her mind already. Funny how what had started out as a mere hobby had become her career. Her dad had given her an old Polaroid when she was ten, and the rest as they say, was history. Now she had her own studio and a full calendar.

Moving things around to accommodate her schedule—particularly during wedding season—hadn't been easy, but definitely worth it. In fact, in her opinion, this Murder Mystery Weekend was the only downside to the entire trip. Once this was over with, they could continue on to more substantial touring. She'd like to visit the Orkneys, see Culloden Battlefield, Doune Castle and Rosslyn Chapel. She wanted to spend more time outdoors, to breathe in more of the air. It had a soft, woodsy flavor to it that sat well on her tongue. She loved the pink thistle blooms and the green, green grass. The way the mountains pushed into the sky and the sky reflected it all back in the lochs. It was so very different from what she was accustomed to, so very lovely in a lush and raw way. She couldn't wait to go through her photos, to see if she'd been able to properly capture what she was seeing.

Steeling herself against the coming evening, they made their way downstairs and found the rest of the "players" in the library. According to the brochure she'd read in order to keep the gathering intimate, they limited participants to twenty. Wine and whiskey were plentiful, and the little sandwich she snatched from a tray only whetted her appetite. She'd been too befuddled to eat—which was strange enough in its own right—when they'd first arrived.

To her unreasonable irritation, she felt her spirits droop when she realized their host was not in the room. Quite honestly, for what this "intimate weekend of murder and mayhem" was costing them per person, she not only expected the host to be readily available, but to cater to their every whim. That was wholly unreasonable, she knew, but that was just the sort of mood she was in.

She wanted to see the man—to know if she was going to have the same extreme reaction to him every time she did—and she hated the fact that he made her feel weird in her own body.

In short, because it suited her to think so, this was all his fault.

The least he could do was show up and put her out of her misery.

At that moment, Cam MacKinnon strode into the

room. A commanding presence, she couldn't help but notice the way he moved—confident yet unhurried with a grace one wouldn't expect from a man of his size. He didn't just inhabit the space around him—he owned it, conquered it, made it conform to his standards. He wore a crisp white dress shirt tucked into a red and green plaid kilt and, though she'd fully expected to see a man in a skirt as completely effeminate, strangely she did not.

In fact, the same meltdown that had accompanied his presence the last time returned in full force. She felt her blood heat beneath her skin, her knees go a little weak and the melting sensation in her womb triggered the instant desire to press her legs together and squirm.

Preferably against him.

Good Lord, what the hell was wrong with her? Summer wondered through a fog of lust. Her ears rung and her mouth alternately watered and parched and once again that dumb-ass smile she couldn't seem to control spread across her lips.

He returned the grin when he saw her and gave her a slow appreciative nod, his eyes lingering hotly on her exposed cleavage. Her traitorous nipples pebbled again. "I knew that outfit would suit you," he said, his burr low and approving. His blue eyes twinkled with something that made her heart race. "You make a fine serving wench, lass."

Before she could form a retort—although she had no idea what she would have said—he moved to the front of the room.

Irrationally, this completely infuriated her and she had the glum premonition she should get used to it where the sexy Scot was concerned.

Equally irrationally, she found it all stupidly thrilling.

And yet she was the one who was supposed to be level-headed? To keep the rest of their party in line?

She had a sneaking suspicion she was going to do a piss poor job of it so long as they were here.

2

HE'D BEEN RIGHT about the outfit, Cam thought as he covertly stared at Summer Davies across the room. He'd delivered his traditional welcome-to-your-murder-party speech and instructed everyone on how the game was to be played. Though they didn't know it, he had a couple of staff members who were pretending to be guests as well and they'd expertly direct the play of the game. He could do his duty as host—his preferred role—and stay out of the drama, so to speak. He loved writing the games, inventing the characters.

Playing them out, however, had never truly been his cup of tea.

His ghillie, surrogate father and best friend, Ramsay, followed his gaze and shook his head. "You're a glutton for punishment, aren't you, lad?"

"I couldn't resist," Cam confessed, chuckling. "Breasts like that deserve to be put on display."

Ramsay's eyes narrowed in disapproval, immediately chastening him. "What if she was Genevieve? How would you feel about it then, eh, boy? If some bloke were messing with her the way you are with this American girl?"

He felt his expression blacken. "That'd be different."

"She's somebody's daughter, somebody's sister, possibly even somebody's wife. Watch yourself, Cam. If you expect the other staff to respect the guests and your 'no fraternization' rule, then you'd better keep to it yourself."

Too true, Cam knew and didn't need the reminder. Before he'd bought this place and started his increasingly profitable murder mystery weekends, which had originally been created to give the stalkers' wives something to do while their husbands looked for deer, he'd been on the wrong end of a sexual harassment suit.

One that had been completely and utterly false.

Not to say that he hadn't been involved with women he'd worked with in the past—he had—but he wouldn't have made a play for Margo MacDonald if she'd been sprinkled with porn star dust and dipped in gold. She was a heinous bitch of the first order and she'd never done anything for him, hadn't found her the least bit attractive. Evidently his lack of interest had hurt her feelings and the careful rebuffs he'd sent in her direction when she'd behaved inappropriately toward him had pissed her off to the point that *she'd* made false allegations against *him* for nothing more than the sheer sport of it.

The company had been a family holding—one of many in MacKinnon Industries—and it had become a very public, very embarrassing ordeal. It didn't matter that she'd been lying, only that one of the MacKinnon sons had been involved. He'd been exonerated, of course—the truth will always out—but he was certain there were still some ignorant people who thought that his name had been what saved him, not the truth.

As a result of the entire ordeal, he'd left the family business and started his own. His parents and siblings had protested fiercely, but Cam hadn't felt right about continuing to work at any of the family holdings after the PR nightmare brought about by the ungrounded suit. He could truthfully say that if there'd been a silver lining at all in the entire mess, it had to be buying this old ruin and making it his home.

Cam cast a proud glance around the room, appreciating the vaulted beamed ceiling, the previously crumbling stone walls covered with tapestries, the slate floor and the enormous fireplace, and felt a tremendous amount of satisfaction bloom in his chest.

It had taken every bit of his savings and retirement to purchase and renovate this old rotting pile of rocks, but he didn't regret a single pound of it. Scotland was riddled with castles, almost all crumbling ruins along lochs, but for whatever reason, this one had said home to him. This one had been the one that had made him feel grounded and at peace. He liked the way the air felt here, the way it settled in his lungs. He'd felt a strange connection to the land it stood on and knew every inch of it by heart now, every stick of timber, every stone, every rise and fall, burn and ridge. The satisfaction of knowing that this was his land—his ground—brought a sense of well-being he'd never accurately been able to describe. He only knew he loved it here, and would fight to the last breath for it if need be.

While there were many struggling estates around the Highlands Cam was proud to say that his wasn't. Ramsay was a first-class ghillie who knew how to take care of the streams and the land, ensuring plenty of fish and game for the outdoorsmen, and they'd renovated many of the crofter's cottages to rent out both to the temporary visitor and the more permanent variety. Between the B&B services, corporate events, stalkers and murder mystery parties, the estate was a profitable enjoyment as well as his home.

He'd be a fool to risk it over a woman, Cam thought, remembering all the hell Margo had caused. It was why he'd always had a no-fraternization policy at Castle MacKinnon, going so far as making the employees sign a commitment to keep to that code.

Guests and coworkers were completely off-limits.

And until Summer Davies had walked through his door with her copper penny curls and dark brown eyes, he hadn't once wished he could break his own rule. Had there been pretty girls? Hundreds. Had he felt a sparkler of attraction? Occasionally. But he'd never, not once, been tempted to act on it.

She more than tempted him.

Over the past several years he'd watched many a woman disembark from a tour bus—it was his first opportunity to scrutinize his guests and consider character assignments, after all—but he'd never had one affect him quite so violently as Ms. Davies. There'd been something about the way she tilted her head toward the sun and the way that same sun had gilded her features. Her keen, observant eyes had methodically scanned her surroundings and the sheer delight—wonder, even—that had shone in her gaze and shaped her smile had been like a sucker punch to his gut. He'd recognized her awe because he'd felt it himself the first time he'd ever set foot on the estate.

Had the intrigue merely stopped there, he might have been fine. But it hadn't. There'd been a more telling physical reaction as well.

He'd gone instantly—shockingly—hard when he'd seen her.

His erection had practically broken the sound barrier it had moved so fast and the urge to back her up against the wall and taste her lips had all but overpowered him.

And the kicker? The irony?

She wanted him just as much. Gratifyingly, she'd actually tottered a bit when she'd seen him, then she'd smiled an adorably self-conscious smile. He'd watched her eyes dilate and her nipples pop out against her shirt and she'd literally licked her own lips while staring at his mouth.

Serious turn-on. He exhaled a slow fatalistic breath.

But Ramsay—his own personal Jiminy Cricket—had been right to remind him that she was off-limits. If he had any chance of keeping these other guys under his employ in line, then he had to keep himself in check, as well. He had to set an example. True, he wanted her more than he'd ever wanted a woman before—she was a definite phenomena—but, ultimately that was just too damned bad.

He watched her covertly tug at the bodice of her dress, a scowl marring her otherwise smooth brow and felt a grin twitch at his lips.

"Did Gladys tell you that Genevieve had called again?" Ramsay asked him.

"No." He frowned. "Do I need to call her back?" More than likely his sister was calling to bemoan the fact that their thick-skulled, living-in-the-dark-ages father still hadn't accepted the fact that none of his sons wanted to take over MacKinnon Holdings so that he could retire. Genevieve, on the other hand, was chomping at the bit to prove herself.

Given the fact that their older brother, Ewan, had just asked their father to let him manage the philanthropy aspect of the company and had informed him that he and his impending bride—an American he'd met on the West Highland Way of all places—would be wandering the world together to provide help where help was needed, their father had to know that his choices were getting more limited by the day. Cam, of course, had already told him that he had no intention of taking the reins, but for reasons which escaped him, he thought his father still harbored a small hope that he'd change his mind.

Hell would freeze over first. His place was here.

He'd actually talked to Alec about the situation yesterday—Alec was even more reluctant to take the business over than he or Ewan, tied as he was to the water—and they'd decided that if their bull-headed father didn't come to his senses soon they'd tag team him with putting Genevieve in charge the next time they all got together. He hoped it didn't come to that. Genevieve, he knew, would rather their father came to the decision on his own.

"She said for you to call her when you got a second, that it wasn't too terribly important."

So he'd been right. She merely wanted to bitch. He'd lend an ear later. For the moment he needed to mingle with his guests…one in particular.

"Cam," Ramsay repeated warningly. "Watch yourself."

He would, of course. But that didn't mean that he had to ignore her completely, Cam thought as he inexplicably made his way across the room to where she stood with the ladies she traveled with. He was the host, after all. It was his job to be hospitable. No ulterior motive, he told himself, knowing it was a lie. He was reluctantly fascinated by her, wanted to hear her speak and secretly hoped he'd find her dull and boring so that he could forget about her and move on. He quickly appraised the group and decided one had to be her mother—same penny curls—and the other... A best friend? An aunt, maybe?

"Good evening, ladies," he said, giving them a little bow. "How do you like our fair castle so far?"

"It's lovely," the one he'd assumed was the mother said. Her smile was genuine—quite lovely, actually— but her eyes were sad. "We're delighted to be here." She extended her hand. "I'm Charlotte Ann Davies, by the way. This is my sister, Mimi, and my daughter, Summer." She gestured to both in turn.

"My pleasure," he said, his gaze lingering on Summer. He couldn't help himself. She had the most interesting face. More intriguing than beautiful, it had character. She had high, wide cheekbones, a slender little nose and a mouth that was naturally pink and equally carnal. "Summer is an interesting name," he said, looking at her. "That's a new one to me. We've had a couple of Autumns come through, but never a Summer."

"She hates her name," the one called Mimi confided, laughing. "Says people always expect her to have a sunny disposition and blond hair."

He laughed and imagined that was true enough.

"Ah. If not sunny, then how would you describe your disposition, Miss Davies?"

She quirked a droll brow. "At the moment? Put-upon."

Her mother gasped. "Summer," she admonished, frowning at her daughter. "No worries, Mr. MacKinnon," she quickly assured him. "She'll get into the spirit of things."

"Or just into the spirits," she said with a significant arch of her brows, then with a nod at her mother and aunt, made a beeline for the whiskey decanter.

Unable to help himself—utterly enchanted—Cam followed her. So much for dull and boring. Perhaps she'd be stupid. "That bad, is it?"

She tossed two fingers of Glenfiddich back and didn't choke like most other Americans. A whiskey drinker, then? Another intriguing tidbit of her character. In his experience, most women preferred wine.

She looked up at him, her expression guarded. "The place? No. It's lovely, picturesque. The dress? Yes. It's utterly revolting and horrid."

He chuckled softly. "It fits well," he said, his gaze dropping to the milky mounds of creamy flesh spilling out of the top. His mouth actually watered.

She put a single finger under his chin and deter-minedly lifted his gaze from her breasts to her eyes. "My face is up here."

"Indeed it is." That's where her lips were, after all, he thought, blinking in an attempt to clear his thoughts. Definitely not stupid then. Oh, hell… "I'm sorry," he said, giving himself a shake. "I'm behaving abomina-bly." And he was. His mother would undoubtedly take a birch to him if she saw the way he was acting around this particular woman. He muttered a low curse and made a concerted effort to focus on her face.

Half of her ripe lips lifted in a smile. "It's boorish, but flattering," she said with a refreshing bit of candor. She aimed another grimace at the dress and then looked up at him. "Nevertheless, if you could do something about this dress, I would be extremely grateful. Also, while you're sorting that out, if I could be one of the characters who is murdered off quickly, that would be great, too."

So she was one of those, was she? Cam thought, smiling down at her. A reluctant participant. He studied her thoughtfully. "You want to get murdered quickly?"

She leaned in as though sharing a confidence and a whiff of her scent teased him, something fruity and warm. It went directly to his groin. "I'd happily die first."

He chuckled, becoming more fascinated with her by the second. "I don't understand. If this wasn't your sort of weekend, then why are you here?" Put-upon, indeed.

She gestured to her mother and aunt across the room, who were engaged in conversation with an Irish couple from Dublin. "Them," she said simply, a hint of sadness in her voice, and that lone note of cheerlessness made him unaccountably uncomfortable, as though his happiness was already—impossibly—tied to hers.

He waited, knowing there was more of an explanation and his patience paid off.

"My father passed away eight months ago," she said and there was a throaty quality to her voice that made him want to console her, to hold her and promise her that things would be all right. As if he had that power, that knowledge, even. "This was supposed to be their trip," she explained. "Instead, Aunt Mimi and I are here."

"I see," he said. So that accounted for the sadness he'd seen in her mother's eyes and Summer's willingness to participate in something she clearly wasn't going to enjoy. He wasn't offended. To each his own. "I'm sure she appreciates your company," he said, for lack of anything better.

There were never quite good enough words to comfort someone with that sort of grief, the loss of a loved one. He knew that the time would eventually come when he'd lose his parents, but a world in which they didn't exist was so wrong he couldn't even contemplate it. Hamish and Mhairi MacKinnon had been married for almost forty years, and ridiculously, enviously in love for as long as he could remember. Had there been the occasional row? Yes, but those had been few and far between, and had burned out as quickly as they'd flared.

"She does appreciate my being here," she said with a nod. "And it was worth it if it makes her happy, helps her grieve."

That was admirable, he would admit, but she'd lost her father. Was she not grieving, too? "And what about you? Will this be good for you?"

She seemed startled by the question, her brown eyes blinking in surprise, as though considering her own needs wasn't customary. "Yes," she said after a moment. "It will be. Has been. We all miss him," she said on a sigh. "But he was my mother's great love. They were inseparable. You never saw one without the other and it's quite odd seeing her alone, as though she was actually part of a set that's been misplaced."

What a sad description, Cam thought, looking at Charlotte Ann Davies again. No doubt seeing her mother's pain only compounded the loss of her father. And witnessing a loved one's ache was almost worse than coping with your own.

"She got a real kick out of this," Summer said, gesturing to her costume. "She kept trying to tell me that I didn't look like an eighteenth-century streetwalker, but couldn't quite keep a straight face."

Back to the dress again, were they? He smiled down at her. "Would you like to change before dinner?"

She breathed a grateful sigh of relief that was almost comical. "Yes, actually, I would. Because I don't know what will happen when I try to sit down." Another droll smile shaped her lips. "I'm assuming you try to keep everything PG here at Castle MacKinnon."

"You'd be correct." Though there was absolutely nothing PG or PC, for that matter, about how he was feeling at the moment. Five minutes in her company and she'd turned him inside out, not to mention thoroughly turned him on. It was insane, sheer madness, and rather than try to avoid going crazy, he seemed hell-bent on facilitating his own destruction.

With equal amounts excitement and dread, he put a finger in the small of her back and nudged her forward. "Come along, then," he told her. "Let's go see what we can find."

Maybe he could locate a nun's habit, Cam thought, because the more of her that was covered up, the better for his state of mind.

And his kilt, which was tenting unbecomingly at the moment.

3

"SO WHAT PART OF THE States do you hail from specifically?" Cam asked her as he directed her toward the costume room.

"Little Cabbage Valley, Kentucky," she said, wondering why this conversation seemed so surreal. Possibly because his fingers were nestled at the small of her back, sending hot shivers up her spine. She could feel the heat rolling off of him in waves and she wanted to absorb it, soak it in, bask in it. It was ridiculous how he affected her—she could feel him in her own blood and with every beat of her heart, the sensation—the bizarre connection—only intensified. It was impossible, she knew, and yet it was happening. Much as it disturbed her to admit it, she was devastatingly attracted to him. To the point where, were he to crook a finger, acceptance was swiftly becoming a foregone conclusion.

He sniggered. "Little Cabbage Valley?"

"Hey, don't laugh," she said, feigning outrage as they made their way down the corridor. Pictures of long-dead ancestors—his? she wondered—looked on from ornate, gilt frames. "We take our cabbage very seriously.

I'll have you know you're talking to a former Cabbage Queen."

He opened a door, then flipped on the light, revealing an entire room devoted to costumes. She spotted fairy wings and a vampire cape, numerous wigs and hats and a glass-fronted cabinet full of jewelry and accessories. "A cabbage queen? *Royal cabbage?* You're having me on."

"I am not," she said, nodding once. "Cabbage is big business in our little valley." And it was true. There were acres and acres of good ground planted with cabbage every year.

He looked adorably confused. "So you're a cabbage farmer then?"

She laughed and shook her head. "No, I'm a photographer, but I have taken more than my fair share of pictures of especially large cabbages. And slaw," she added as an afterthought. And she couldn't begin to count the babies she'd shot in hollowed-out cabbages, the diaper-clad newborns nestled in the larger, outer leaves.

A perplexed line emerged between his brows and he studied her as if he still wasn't altogether convinced that she was being truthful. "I'm not even going to ask," he said grimly. He walked over to a section of the huge room and pointed to a narrow rack against the wall. "This is our serving wench section," he told her. "You may choose any costume that suits your fancy."

"What if I don't want to be a serving wench?" she asked, just to be contrary. "What if I want to be a duchess?"

He blinked. "I thought you wanted to die early."

"I do." She pulled a blue costume from the rack and

held it up to her body. She liked the color, but the bodice was still cut too low. She grimaced, wondering if all serving wenches were of such low moral character, or only the ones here at Castle MacKinnon.

"Then stick with the serving wench." He smiled down at her, making her belly go fluttery. Warmth tickled her traitorous nipples and wound its way to her womb. She didn't know what sort of cologne he was wearing, but it smelled divine. Like musk and fresh cut grass. "Alas, she will be tragically murdered tomorrow at lunch."

"Did she see something she wasn't supposed to?"

"You'll have to play the game to find out."

"Well, surely she doesn't die for no reason."

"Everyone has their secrets," he said mysteriously. "What you need to be asking yourself is why anyone would want to murder the serving wench."

"Prinny probably didn't like her dress," she said, eliciting a laugh from her host.

He pulled a yellow gown from the rack. "Try this one," he said, handing it to her. "It's summery."

She smiled sweetly. "But it doesn't match my disposition."

His keen blue gaze skimmed over her, leaving a hot trail of gooseflesh in its wake. "Yes, but the shade looks nice with your hair."

Incredibly, she blushed at the compliment. She hadn't so much as batted a lash when he'd admired her breasts earlier, but a simple statement about her hair and she turned color? What the hell was wrong with her? What was it about this man, in particular, that was causing such turmoil?

"Are you okay, Summer?" he asked, an incorrigible knowing grin on his face. "You look a little warm."

Wretch. It was almost as though he could hear the rapid beat of her heart, could sense the heat he was firing in her blood. She could tell from the smile in his voice that he knew exactly what was wrong with her.

Him.

He rattled her. And that was putting it mildly.

"I prefer the blue," she lied, returning the yellow to the rack. She'd figure out a way to deal with the cleavage issue.

His blue eyes twinkled and he shrugged his massive shoulders. "Suit yourself."

"I'd like to take some pictures while I'm here," she said, trying to distract herself. "Do you have any objection?"

He shook his head. "Not at all. Take as many as you like."

Excellent. Getting out of the house would get her away from him and she suspected that, despite what her melting, burning, desperate body was telling her, she needed to put some distance between them. The last thing she needed was a short-lived affair with a Scottish giant who made her wish she wasn't so practical. This could go nowhere—they lived on two different continents—and she'd never mastered the art of indulging her body without her heart becoming involved. Though if there had ever been a guy who made her want to try, then he was certainly it.

"I saw the folly on the drive over," she told him. "I'd really like to get a few shots of that."

"Of course. I'd be happy to go with you, show you the grounds."

Sort of defeated the purpose of trying to get away

from him, didn't it? "Er…thanks, but your ghillie has already offered."

"He has, has he?" Cam asked and, though he smiled, it didn't look quite so pleasant. "How kind of him." Definitely annoyed. How odd. "But I am certain that Ramsay will be busy with the stalkers. That's his job, after all. Besides, who better to show you the place than me, the owner and host?"

He was being downright proprietary, Summer thought, studying him thoughtfully. Under ordinary circumstances his attitude would have irritated her, but instead she was secretly pleased. Which was stupid, all things considered, but she couldn't seem to help herself.

"Won't you be busy with the murder party?"

His gaze lingered over her breasts once more and she felt her breathing hitch in her chest at the blatant approval she saw in his disconcertingly frank gaze. "We'll have some free time. After lunch tomorrow then?"

"I don't want to monopolize all of your time," she said, lying once again. Because, despite knowing she should avoid him, presently she'd like nothing better than to monopolize the living hell out of him. Preferably until her toes curled and her eyes rolled back in her head. Clearly she'd lost her mind.

He inclined his head. "I'm yours to command."

Summer chuckled darkly. "Oh, I sincerely doubt that, but in that case I'd like you to get out." Cam MacKinnon was a leader of men, not a follower and she knew damned well if she gave him a command, he'd do just the opposite out of sheer obstinacy. How did she know that? Who knew? But she did all the same.

He blinked. "What?"

She shooed him with her hand and gestured toward the blue dress. "I need to change." *I need to breathe and you're using all my oxygen.* He was just so huge, so larger than life.

So…male.

"In here? Right now?"

She swallowed an exasperated sigh. "Dinner is in five minutes and I forgot to lay a trail of bread crumbs back to my room, so yes, in here."

He smiled at her and there was something quite thrillingly predatory about that grin. "I'll guard the door for you."

Her heart skipped a beat and her mouth went bone dry. "And they say chivalry is dead."

"Fluent in smart-ass, I see," he said, nodding approvingly. "I like that in a woman." And with that, he finally, blessedly, slipped outside.

Shaking from the exchange with him—strangely exhilarated despite the need pounding away at her common sense—Summer smiled and reached around to snag the zipper…only to realize it was annoyingly out of reach.

Damn.

"Everything all right?" he called through the door. He had probably known all along that she was going to need help, the opportunistic sexy beast. She didn't know whether to laugh or scream.

Mortified and irritated at her own lack of foresight— after all, she'd needed her mother to get into the blasted thing—she made her way to the door. "No, actually. I could use a little help."

He opened the door with rapid speed and a hopeful smile, peering into the room. "Really? How so?"

He was well and truly rotten and curiously, that made him all the more appealing. She chewed her tongue. "The zipper," she said. "If you can just get it started."

Careful to close the door behind him, he slipped back into the room. "Of course. Turn 'round."

She did and waited, the anticipation of his touch making her stomach flutter. She loved the husky burr of his voice, could feel his heat and hesitation and, strangely, it was the latter that affected her the most. The first brush of his warm fingers against her back made her breathing hitch and her knees weaken. It was ridiculous how much she wanted this complete stranger. How much she wanted to thread her fingers through his dark auburn curls and see how the whiskey he'd drunk earlier tasted against her tongue. He was a rogue of the first order— not usually her type because rogues weren't as easily managed—and yet she couldn't seem to help herself.

Something about him triggered all kinds of primal urges, ones she'd never even dreamed she possessed. She felt his breath against the back of her neck and knew that he'd moved closer and it took every ounce of strength she possessed not to lean into him, to sink against him. He carefully lowered the zipper down to the back of her bra, then just as carefully retreated.

"You can get it from there, I think," he said, his voice gratifyingly unsteady. "I'll wait outside."

"No need," she said, needing a little time to compose herself. "I can find my way to the dining room."

He released a slight sigh and his lips twitched with knowing amusement. "Maybe so, lass, but you'll need to be zipped into the other one."

She squeezed her eyes shut and swore hotly under her breath.

He chuckled, the sound soft and low. Impossibly sexy. "What was that?"

"Nothing." She turned to glare at him, more out of sorts than she was used to being. "You're really enjoying this, aren't you?"

He crossed his arms over his massive chest and rocked back on his heels. "Now that's one of those damned if I do and damned if I don't kind of questions, isn't it? If I say that I'm not enjoying it, then you're going to know I'm lying. But if I say I am, then I'm a cad." He essayed a grin. "Either way, I'm in danger of losing your good opinion."

She clutched the sagging dress to her chest and quirked a pointed brow. "That's begging the assumption you ever had it to start with."

Seemingly impressed, he smiled wider. "Then I'll just have to try harder. Let me know when you need me." He ducked out once more.

Let me know when you need me? If that were her only criteria, then it was met *now*. She needed him *now*. Hot, hard and fast, his spectacular body her playground, that beautiful masculine mouth feeding at hers, his big hands mapping her body, testing the feel of her against his palms. But need wasn't all that had to be considered and she suspected that the reason her body had developed such a craving was because her subconscious recognized a deeper connection—an inherent trust that couldn't be explained. That was the trouble with fire—it burned—and she wasn't in any position to handle the blisters at the moment. This trip was for her mother. She'd do well to remember that.

She shimmied out of the dress and quickly stepped into the other one. Much better, Summer thought. Much less cleavage. Plenty of thick, sturdy fabric to conceal her recalcitrant nipples. She managed the zipper to just above her bra and, after jumping around trying to get it fully closed without his assistance, finally conceded defeat.

"Cam?" she hissed quietly.

Once again he eagerly entered the room. His gaze did a lazy perusal from one end of her body to the other, leaving a sizzling sensation in its wake. Pity serving wenches didn't carry fans. She could use one about now.

Moving her hair out of the way, she reluctantly presented her back to him. With a deft touch he located the zipper and tugged it gently into place, his fingers lingering for a bit too long.

"We'd better get to the dining room," she said. Did that breathless voice belong to her? Geez, Lord.

"Yes," he said thoughtfully, a curiously grim note in his deep, resonate burr. "Before I forget myself and do something spectacularly stupid. Like kiss you."

4

SINCE CAM HAD GIVEN her the go-ahead on taking pictures, Summer had taken him at his word and was documenting this weekend right along with the rest of the trip to go into the scrapbook she planned to put together for her mother and aunt for Christmas. Though she'd initially only intended to take photos of her family, she soon found herself taking shots of the other participants.

The lavish costumes set against the backdrop of the castle made for interesting photographs and she just couldn't seem to help herself. She planned to get the addresses for each of the participants and send them copies when it was done.

One subject, in particular, had captured her attention and when she counted her photos she was stunned to realize that she'd taken *sixteen* of a certain sexy Scot.

But how could she not, when he looked like that? Take now, for instance. He and Ramsay were standing in the broad dining room doorway, apparently in a tense exchange. One that, given the occasional looks in her direction, she was an unwitting party to. Summer felt her lips twitch as she ladled up another spoonful of savory leek soup. If she had her guess, the ghillie had come to take her to the folly as promised and Cam was heading him off at the pass.

Looking grim-faced but beaten, Ramsay made his way to her side. "Cam will be escorting you this afternoon in my stead," the older gentleman told her. "I hope you don't mind."

She looked over his shoulder at Cam, who was watching them with interest. "Not at all," she told him, smiling to put his mind at ease. Her belly gave a little flutter at the thought of being alone with him again, particularly after his kissing-her-would-be-spectacularly-stupid remark last night. "I'm sure Mr. MacKinnon will make an excellent guide."

Ramsay ignored her comment. "It's better from a horse's back. Do you ride?"

She nodded once. "Passably." She lived in Kentucky Derby country—it was a prerequisite.

"I'll saddle Esmerelda up for you then."

He straightened and gave Cam a dark look as he brushed past him. Cam merely smiled—his usual expression, she'd noticed—and met her gaze. He gave his head a tiny jerk toward the door, silently beckoning her.

Such a small gesture, utterly loaded with temptation. She couldn't begin to imagine how many women had succumbed to the smile, the little inviting tilt of his auburn head.

And fool that she was—knowing that she was only half-heartedly clinging to a slippery slope—she got up.

"Where are you going?" Mimi asked, garnering the

attention of everyone seated at the dining room table. Their gazes swung to her expectantly.

"To take pictures of the estate," she said. Which was true. So why did it feel like a lie? Why did this feel more like a date? Like a sneaky liaison?

Her aunt's brow creased with bafflement. "But we're going to play Clue in the library."

Considering a colonic cleanse preferable to playing Clue in the library, Summer didn't even pretend to ponder the alternative. She twinkled her fingers at her aunt, bent down and kissed her mother—who seemed to be enjoying herself more here than at any other stop—and made her getaway.

She bolted from the room fast enough to make Cam chuckle. "Do you dislike all games in general or is it just Clue you object to?"

"Neither, but given the choice between playing a game or taking pictures, I'm going to choose the camera every time."

He led her down the hall to the kitchen, snagged a basket from the big working table and a kiss from the cook—Ramsay's wife, she discerned—then led her toward the back door. She barely had time to appreciate the dried herbs and copper cookware hanging from the ceiling or the aroma of fresh baking bread.

Cam held the door open for her and the brisk wind made her eternally thankful that she'd brought her lined, weather-proof jacket. "Is the camera always your first choice then?" he wanted to know, seeming genuinely curious about her.

She took a deep breath and imagined she could taste the heather. Lord, it was beautiful here. She couldn't imagine another spot on earth as beautiful. "Most of the time."

He tsked under his breath and gave his head a woeful shake. "Lucky camera. It's a bit of a walk to the barn, so we'll take the cart," he said, stowing the basket in the back.

Summer climbed in next to him and wondered how she could be simultaneously wound tight and utterly relaxed at once.

Because she was.

Every nerve ending thrummed with sexual energy— just looking at his hands made her imagine them against her naked flesh, the ruddy shade contrasting with her pale skin—and the throbbing ache in her womb intensified every second she spent in his presence.

Conversely, she felt at peace here in this place with him, as though she'd blindly wandered into a second home she wasn't even aware she had. She loved the rolling hills, the heather, thistles and sheep that dotted the landscape. The mist that hung on the mountains, the same mountains reflected in the loch. It was beyond beautiful to her.

"You're smiling," he noted.

She was, she realized. Summer released a breath. "I like it here," she said. "It's new but familiar. How bizarre is that?"

A strange look flitted over his face. "That's the exact feeling I got when I first saw the place," he confessed. "The house was practically falling in, the estate had gone to ruin…and yet I knew it was home. The land had an immediate hold on me and I've taken root. I bought it, knowing that keeping it in the black would require a lot of creative financing and potential hair loss, but have never regretted it. Not once."

So he went with his gut, Summer thought, recognizing the trait because it was hers as well. She actually had a criminal justice degree—she liked the idea of order—but much to her parents' chagrin had never used it. She'd hung up her photography shingle and never looked back. In the end, it had been the best decision. She couldn't imagine being stuffed inside an office all day. She needed to move, to feed her creativity. Granted she could lose hours in the dark room at her house, but that was almost therapeutic, for lack of a better description. There was something about watching the film develop and, although she adored her digital camera and appreciated the technology, there were times when good old-fashioned film was best.

He drew to a stop at the barn, a large gray-stone structure that was as beautiful as it was functional. Ramsay moved forward, a lead in each hand. She knew instantly which horse belonged to Cam. It was a giant black beast that pawed the ground, snorted angrily and fought the bit.

"Your animal is in a snit," Ramsay told him. "Settle down!" he snarled at the horse, giving the reins a threatening rattle.

Hers, thank God, did not appear to be in bad humor. The mare was a dappled gray that put her in mind of mother of pearl and she seemed to be eyeing the black horse with weary disdain.

"Ah, Harley's just mad because I didn't ride him yesterday." Cam pulled a sugar cube from his pocket and fed it to the enormous beast. "Aren't ya, big fella?" he crooned, stroking his velvety nose.

"Harley?" she asked, chuckling.

"My mother threatened to disown me if I bought a motorcycle, so I got the horse instead and named him after it. I always wanted a Harley." He grinned his roguish grin. "Now I've got one."

"Thinks he's got a sense of humor, he does," Ramsay muttered. "Bloody beast ought to be named Satan. He's the devil incarnate is what he is," the older man groused.

Summer stifled another laugh, thankful that Esmerelda seemed like such a docile creature by comparison. Ramsay led her over to the block and held the mare so Summer could mount. "Unlike this one," he said fondly. "She's an absolute angel, she is." He looked up at her. "You won't have a bit of trouble with her at all, lass."

Summer settled into the saddle and took the reins. "Thanks, Ramsay."

She watched Cam put a foot in the stirrups and swing easily onto Harley's back. The animal gave a threatening jolt and his ears lay back, but a bit of whispering from Cam and a firm hand on the reins and the animal settled. He looked completely natural, completely confident and completely sexy. His auburn curls glinted in the early afternoon sun and that damned endearing dimple bisected his cheek, making her heart melt and her thighs quiver. His were big and muscled and beautiful, not much unlike the animal he currently rode, and in a moment of sheer prophetic insight, she knew she would know him in the biblical sense before the weekend was out.

Spectacularly stupid? Oh, yeah. But…inevitable all the same. How could she have possibly thought she could resist him? How could she have possibly imagined that she would cling to logic and common sense in light of the unbelievable attraction between them? Particularly when she'd never felt this way before? When she'd never wanted a man—literally ached for one—the way she did Cam MacKinnon.

Crazy? Insane? Reckless?

Most definitely…but that wasn't going to stop her.

He looked over at her, seemed to be taking her measure. "You ready to ride?"

Summer swallowed a hysterical laugh. Oh, yeah. More than he knew.

5

"How long have you lived here?" Summer asked him, her tone suggesting that she was preoccupied framing another shot. He looked over and smiled when he realized he'd been right. They'd ridden along the loch, through a small portion of the forest and had finally arrived at the folly. He'd lost count of how many pictures she'd taken, but could tell by the relaxed and pleasant expression on her face that she was thoroughly enjoying herself.

He took a ridiculous amount of pleasure from that.

"I've been here four years," Cam told her.

"And does your family live nearby?"

"About sixty miles south," he said. "I've got two brothers and a sister. My family owns MacKinnon Holdings, an import-export business and, while I contributed long enough to net the capital to buy this place, ultimately I wanted something that was my own, something that I built from the ground up. Success or failure, but at least it was mine, you know?" And that was true, if not the whole story. He smiled and gestured to the folly and surrounding grounds. "This was a gamble, but I love it and don't regret the choices I've made. This is where I belong, where my heart is."

He dismounted, tethered his horse to a tree, then walked over and helped her down. She slid slowly along his body until her feet touched the ground, and when she looked up he was struck anew at her perfection. She had the creamiest skin he'd ever seen, and her dark chocolate eyes and sooty lashes stood out in sharp relief. She had a tiny freckle next to her mouth and he was suddenly consumed with the idea of touching his tongue to it— tasting it and her. More than just desire was at work here, Cam thought, and the knowledge made an uneasy sensation prickle in his chest.

Her breathing grew shallow and her gaze settled on his lip. He watched her swallow, observed the muscle movement in the slim column of her throat. Her pulse fluttered wildly there, an I-want-you tattoo through her veins that he didn't have to hear because he could see.

Damn.

Why hadn't he listened to Ramsay? Why had he insisted that he would take her here? Alone to this secluded spot? He'd nearly kissed her yesterday. Had wanted nothing better than to spin her sexy little ass right back into the costume room, lift her skirt and debauch her from one end of the enormous closet to the other.

He'd dreamed about doing just that last night, had subjected himself to a hand job and a cold shower at two in the morning because he hadn't been able to get the shape of her mouth, the sweet swell of her breasts, out of his mind.

She was smart and sassy, with a quick acerbic wit, and just looking at her filled him with intense desire and a strange happiness.

He wanted her.

And it suddenly didn't matter that he'd only met her, that she was a guest, that he should keep his hands off her. Intuition told him the risk was worth the reward and this was a hill he was fully committed to dying on.

He had to have her, knew a part of his soul would die if he didn't.

Cam ran his thumb over her bottom lip. "Do you have any idea how much I want to kiss you right now?"

Her eyes widened, then warmed. She released a shaky breath. "Wouldn't that be 'spectacularly stupid'?"

"On more levels than you can imagine," he said, laughing at the craziness of the situation. "You're a guest in my home. I'm not supposed to hit on you."

She looked up at him from a sweep of dark lashes. "What if I were to hit on you?"

He felt his heart stutter. "I've rebuffed many an advance over the years."

"Did you want to?"

He leveled his gaze at her, wanting to make sure that she understood, knew she was unique, special. "Every single time."

She absorbed that. "And now?"

He chuckled darkly and pointed to the front of his jeans. "That's not a gun, but I can assure you it's ready to fire."

A smile twitched at her lips and her eyes twinkled. "How's your aim?"

He chuckled low. "I *never* miss the target."

"In that case, you should tether Esmerelda—" she

started toward the folly, then slowed and threw a wicked grin over her shoulder "—and get ready to unholster your weapon."

SUMMER DIDN'T HAVE any idea where the bravado was coming from, but was enjoying it entirely too much to overthink it. In fact, she'd decided that she wasn't going to think about this at all. What was the point, really? She instinctively knew that Cam was different—if for no other reason that she wanted him more than she'd ever wanted a man before. She'd taken one look into his glorious eyes and had nearly fallen over. *That* had never happened to her before. And she instinctively knew it was never going to happen again. She'd be a fool to miss this chance. To not enjoy what would be this small chapter in her history. Did it come with risk? Most definitely. But she was prepared to face the consequences.

In short, she was going to borrow a phrase from Nike and just do it.

Because she wanted to. Because it felt right. She'd worry about everything else later. Right now she wasn't going to anticipate regret, not when every fiber of her being was humming with sexual energy, with the need to feel this man between her legs. To make him as crazy for her as she was for him. To make him beg.

He walked up the folly steps and dropped the basket and blanket he'd been carrying on Harley's back onto one of the padded lounge chairs in the little building. If there had ever been a place made for making love, then this was certainly it. Secluded and fanciful, with gently curving arches and roman columns, it was romantic and beautiful.

Given their conversation, she'd thought she'd be the

one to initiate this, but thrillingly, he took one smolder-ing look at her and moved in. Their mouths met as though they were waging war, their tongues seeking and retreating, the kiss more frantic and desperate than anything she'd ever experienced before.

Her nipples pearled, her sex wept and the clothes she was wearing became increasingly irritating because they kept her from feeling him. She tugged at his shirt, desperate to have his muscled body beneath her hands. He was big and hard and thrilling and she ached for him more than she'd ever ached before. Need hammered through her veins, making her crazy with desire. She suckled his lip, tasting him and sighed with pleasure as his big hand cupped her breast, thumbing her nipple through the fabric. She tore impatiently at his clothes, and he took the silent hint.

A moment later, they were both naked, wrapped in the tartan blanket he'd had the foresight to bring and his hot mouth was feeding on her breast, suckling, biting as his hand slid over her belly and between her curls.

The first brush of his fingers against her sent her back arching off the chair, pushing herself against him. She felt like she was already falling apart and was looking forward to her ultimate destruction. Pleasure burned through her, tingling in every nerve ending, thrum-ming in every frenzied, sluggish beat of her heart. He felt wonderful, perfect, better than she could have ever imagined.

She reached down and wrapped her hand around him, stroked him. Hot, slippery skin moved against her palm and she stroke the smooth head, swirling a bit of its moisture around the engorged top. He was hard, so hard…and so big. This was no snub-nosed revolver, that was for damned sure. More like a .357 Magnum. An ill-timed snicker escaped before she could stop herself and she felt him tense above her.

"The last thing any man wants to hear when a woman has got his cock in her hand is a laugh, lass. Would you mind telling me what you find so bloody funny?"

She shared her analogy and had the pleasure of watching him roar with laughter. His blue eyes twinkled. "As nice as it is to hear that my gun's got a decent-size barrel, as it were, if you're thinking that much, then I'm not doing my job right." He put on a condom—thank God, he'd been prepared—then nudged her nether folds. She inhaled sharply as he pushed fully into her. "Ahhhhh," he sighed as though he'd just entered heaven. "Bull's-eye."

Then he began to move and she discovered he was right—she had been thinking too much.

Hot male flesh, smooth, sleek muscle. Coarse masculine hair abrading her nipples.

She drew her legs back, wrapped them even tighter around him and met him thrust for thrust, arching to meet each perfect invasion into her body. He wrapped an arm about her waist, pulling her even more tightly against him, aligning her so that he brushed her clit with every stroke. It swelled with the attention and she felt the first flash of release sparkle in her womb, a little flicker of impending orgasm alerting the rest of her body to brace itself, to get ready for pleasure.

She reached around him and stroked the back of his dick, massaged his stiffened balls and felt a surge of feminine satisfaction when she watched his lips peel away from his teeth and his eyes glaze over. She tweaked one of his nipples, then bent forward and lightly bit his neck. He angled deep, pressed hard…

One, two, three powerful strokes…

And she fractured.

Her back bowed off the chair, every muscle went rigid and her mouth opened in a long soundless scream.

His was not soundless. He roared and shuddered above her, like a Highland warrior, and when her breathing finally returned to normal and the last of the orgasm had rippled out of her, Summer knew that she would not ever, for one minute, regret this.

In fact, she'd only regret it if they didn't get to do it more.

He rolled over as best he could, discarded the condom and settled her firmly against his muscled chest. She felt the oddest sense of homecoming, as though this niche had been made with her in mind. His fingers stroked her hair and he pressed a kiss at her temple. A peace and contentment so deep and unpolluted that it was almost unnerving settled over her and she smiled, savoring the moment. "You're an excellent marksman, Cam MacKinnon."

She felt him chuckle. "You're one helluva target, Summer Davies."

6

BEING SPECTACULARLY STUPID felt spectacularly wonderful, Cam thought as he watched Summer shrug back into her tiny lacy bra. He'd seen every inch of her magnificent body—and committed it to memory—and yet she shyly turned her back to him as she redressed. Silly woman. He could paint her breasts from memory, could still taste them against his tongue.

Cam sighed long and deeply and then smacked his hands against his thighs and said exactly what he was thinking. "I don't know about you, but I feel infinitely better."

Her startled gaze swung to his and she chuckled throatily. "I should hope so, all things considered," she replied drolly.

He chuckled. "No, I mean I've been wanting to do that since I first set eyes on you and now it's almost like—"

"You can think," she supplied, an understanding in her pretty brown eyes.

He grinned. "Exactly."

She hummed under her breath and chewed the inside

of her cheek. "You've taken that gnawing edge off, lifted the veil of lust from your brain and now you're ready to settle in and get to know me? You feel like you can breathe again?"

This honesty was intensely refreshing. Impressed, he studied her thoughtfully. "Yes."

She laughed significantly. "Been there, done that, bought the T-shirt."

An unhappy thought struck and he tried to sound off-hand. "How many times have you bought this particular shirt?"

Her twinkling brown eyes met his. "Well, I'm obviously not a virgin."

Yes, he'd gathered that much he'd not been her first. But was what nagging him at the moment was the undertone to this conversation. He wanted to be special, dammit. He wanted her to tell him that she'd never felt this way before, that she'd never wanted a man as much as she'd wanted him. He felt his eyes widen and he smothered a gasp. Dear God, he was thinking like a woman. Where was this uncertainty coming from? What did it matter if she'd bedded every man from one end of Scotland to the other? She wasn't his and this wasn't even permanent. She was passing through, leaving tomorrow as a matter of fact.

Tomorrow?

His gaze swung to hers once more and a bizarre little dart of panic fluttered through his chest. *Tomorrow?* How could that be right? He'd only just tasted her, just enjoyed the appetizer as it were. He wanted to feast on her, then have her again for dessert.

"Nevertheless," she said, her voice slightly unsure. "This is the first time I've bought this particular shirt.

When I saw it, I had to have it. I couldn't have walked away from it if I'd tried." She swallowed, tucking an errant curl behind her ear. "That's never happened to me before."

The pleasure he took from that admission should have rung a warning bell loud enough to wake the dead, but Cam made himself deliberately deaf. He grinned and peered up at her. "Is that right?"

"Stop fishing," she told him. "I fell instantly in lust with you and you know it. You're about as subtle as a sledgehammer, you know."

"And my head is as thick as an anvil, but you wanted my body anyway." He sighed dramatically, as though being the object of her lust was a burden more than a boon. "You find me irresistible."

"Keep it up," she said, rolling her eyes. "You're quickly losing your appeal."

"That would be tragic, particularly since I wanted to secret you away to one of the turret bedrooms and ravish you all night long."

"You've got a murder mystery to host," she said, her smile giving her away. He wasn't the only one who enjoyed being wanted. "Prinny's mistresses have more people to murder, more paste jewels to steal. My aunt really wants a bottle of poison, by the way," she added, shooting him a smile.

"I'll see what I can do," Cam told her. "The mystery will be resolved by nine—"

"It's Veronica, the opera singer, isn't it? She wants him all to herself."

"—and I'll have the rest of the evening to practice my aim on you. And no, it's not Veronica."

"Beatrice then? She's got a mean look about her."

"That's unkind," Cam told her, laughing. "And no, not Beatrice, either."

"Won't your staff suspect something? If you vanish with me?"

A niggle of unease nudged his belly, but he ignored it. He wrapped his arms around her waist and drew her to him. "Protecting my virtue, are you, lass? Sweet, but unnecessary. We'll be sneaky."

"Ultimately, you're the boss. Is there really a need to be?"

Though he didn't like to discuss this with anyone, he didn't hesitate in telling her. For reasons which escaped him, he wanted to confide in her, knew he could trust her. "Due to an unfortunate bogus sexual harassment suit when I was still with the family company, yes," he said. "We've got a strict no-fraternization rule. Employees aren't allowed to date each other, much less the guests. I'm supposed to set an example."

She inclined her head. "Ahh."

"I can assure you that I did not—"

She stopped him. "Cam, you don't have to assure me."

"But I want to. I need you to—"

"No, I mean I believe you." She gave him a smile.

He blinked. "You believe me? I've been shamelessly flirting with you since you got here, foisted a revealing dress upon you so that I could get a better look at your breasts and *you* believe me?"

She chuckled, the sound soft and throaty. "Yes, I do," she insisted. "In the first place, you're gorgeous. You don't have to *harass* anyone to get them into bed. You just crook a finger."

He peered down at her. "You are exceedingly good for my ego."

"And secondly…" She shrugged. "You're just not the type. Any man who would break ranks with the family business to have something of his own rather than benefit from someone else's success wouldn't do that."

This woman understood him better in less than twenty-four hours than some of his life-long friends. It was as wonderful as it was terrifying. He swallowed, feeling strangely out of sorts. "Thank you," he said. "You can't know what that means to me. It's a dirty stain upon my character, you see, and I feel the constant need to defend it."

"Stop," she told him. "It's unnecessary. And you're letting the vindictive bitch win. I'm assuming she wanted to play with you and you moved your toys to another sandbox?"

He laughed at her analogy. "Something like that, yes."

"That makes my blood boil," she said. "People like her make it harder for those who are being genuinely harassed to get any sort of justice."

"True," he said, with an eye toward the sun. He winced. "As much as I hate to say it, we'd better start heading back. We've both got to get into costume."

Summer groaned. "I can't believe you killed me at lunch and have given me another part for dinner."

He gathered everything they'd brought, then laced his fingers together and helped her mount. She swung easily onto Esmerelda's back. "You said you wanted to be a duchess," he reminded her. He checked her stirrups and tightened the saddle. "You're going to love her part. She's a drunken flirt with a juicy secret."

Summer rolled her eyes. "Where on earth do you find these games?" she asked.

After settling into his own saddle, he gave Harley a nudge a gentle. "I write them, of course."

He had the pleasure of watching her jaw go slack and her eyes round with shock. "You write them? Yourself?"

"Yes. It's entertaining."

Looking mystified, she shook her head. "You are a man of many talents, Mr. MacKinnon."

He waggled his brows suggestively. "And just think, I'm going to show you a whole lot more tonight."

7

LOOKING IMPOSSIBLY SEXY in his kilt again, Cam stood at the front of the room and nodded his thanks as everyone applauded. The murder had been solved, the culprit dragged off to the Tower and the castle was once again safe. As for the duchess and her juicy secret? She was carrying Prinny's secret love child.

Cam MacKinnon had a very vivid imagination.

Summer wandered forward with her mother and aunt to thank Cam for the evening. Actually, she'd be thanking him again in just a few minutes with much more enthusiasm, but her companions didn't need to know that. Not that her mother or aunt would object—they'd actually hoped for a little romance for her on this trip—but telling them about Cam was another matter altogether.

"Thank you so much for such a wonderful evening, Mr. MacKinnon," her mother said, the best smile Summer had seen on her face in a long time wreathing her cheeks. "My late husband would have loved this."

It was true, Summer knew. Much like Cam, she suddenly realized, her dad had had a flair for the dramatic.

He would have embraced his role with enthusiasm—he would have made an excellent Prinny, as a matter of fact—and made it all the more fun for her mother. She felt a twinge of guilt that she hadn't participated with a little more interest herself, but knew that her aunt had picked up her slack. Mimi had barely touched her bubble wrap, Summer had noticed, and had seemed to purposely avoid the alcohol.

Cam's gaze skittered past hers before resting on her mother's. "I genuinely regret that I didn't get to meet him," he said, smiling. "But he was a lucky man to have the three of you in his life."

For the first time in months, her mother's smile actually reached her eyes. Summer's throat tightened. "He would have agreed with you."

"Hasn't this just been wonderful?" Mimi enthused. "I've had the best time. And this castle is simply amazing. All these drafty old rooms and tapestries. I feel like I'm in a Jane Austen novel," she trilled, taking another sip of her drink.

So did she, Summer thought. Only the hero wasn't going to make a bold declaration for her hand and the heroine was going to get on a motorized luxury coach at the end of the book. The thought depressed her much more than it should have, made her want to curl into a ball and sob.

She was being completely irrational. She'd only just met him. How could he be anything more than a holiday fling? A vacation romance? What were the chances that she'd actually meet the love of her life here? In Scotland? A half a world away from the place she called home. Away from her business, away from her family, away from everything familiar.

And yet if Cam asked her to stay with him, there wasn't a doubt in her mind that she'd do it.

The silent admission shook her.

Clearly she had lost her mind because that, more than anything, would be *spectacularly stupid*.

"Are you all right, dear?" her mother asked. Concern lined her brow. "You're looking a little pale."

"I've just got a bit of a headache," she lied. Impending heartache was much more accurate. "I think I'll go ahead and go up to bed."

Her mother laid her hand upon her arm, staying her with a touch. "Thank you for doing this with me, Summer. Coming on this trip. I know that you didn't want to miss work and that rearranging your schedule was a trial, but I am so glad that you made this trip with me." She frowned thoughtfully, as though searching for the right words. "I can't shake the feeling that we were supposed to do this, that it was somehow meant to be." She shook her head and smiled self-consciously. "Sounds foolish, doesn't it?"

Summer squeezed her hand. "Not at all, Mom. In fact, I believe you're right."

Her mother tilted her head toward Cam. "Mr. MacKinnon sure seems taken with you," she observed shrewdly. "He hasn't been able to tear his eyes off you all evening."

Summer looked away and felt herself blush.

"Your father used to look at me that way, too. Feels nice, doesn't it?"

She swallowed. "It's flattering."

"Pity we leave in the morning," her mother remarked. "I get the feeling you like him, as well."

Like wasn't nearly a strong enough word. She laughed,

because she didn't know what else to do. "He's an incredible guy," she said. And he was. He was brilliant and funny, incorrigible and shameless and she adored every wickedly wonderful aspect of his character. With just the smallest bit of encouragement she could so easily fall in love with him.

If she hadn't already.

From the corner of her eye, she saw Cam slip from the room and, more aware now more than ever that their time was nearly up, she bid her mother a distracted good-night and made her way out into the hall.

She'd barely taken two steps, when he swooped her up into his arms, then kissed her like his life depended on it. "I've been wanting to do that all evening," he said, his brogue more pronounced with his passion.

She framed his face with her hands, feeling the auburn stubble abrade her palms. "Good," she said. "Because I've wanted you to."

"THE BEST PART ABOUT being lord of the manor is knowing where all the secret passages are," he told her, darting quickly through a hidden door. He hurried up the stairs, then paused to kiss her and catch his breath before mounting the final circular stretch that would take them to their ultimate destination. He'd come up earlier and made up the bed, laid a fire, lit candles and prepared refreshments. He'd wanted everything to be perfect for her.

Unfortunately, he didn't think he was going to be able to wait long enough to allow her the time to appreciate it. He wanted her now. Had to have her now. Though there was too much fabric and buttons and whatnot associated with these costumes, he had to admit they knew how to set a man's blood afire. He couldn't think about the dress for wanting to take it off, couldn't contemplate a button without wanting to slip it from its closure. He couldn't wait to lift her skirt, then his kilt and bury himself in the sleek, dark heat between her thighs.

He mounted the last stair, nudged open the door, then took three strides and laid her down on the bed. Her breasts popped up over the neckline and he feasted on them, savoring one nipple then the next. He groaned against her, felt her sweet questing little hands against his scalp, urging him on.

"Cam," she breathed. "What have you got on under your plaid?"

"Not a damned stitch."

"Then that makes two of us," she panted.

It took a second for her meaning to penetrate, but when it did he laughed wickedly. "Oh, you are a naughty, naughty wench."

"Watch yourself," she told him breathlessly. "I'm a duchess now, remember?"

He found the hem of her dress and lifted it up, then slid a hand up her thigh.

Bare.

He hardened to the point of pain.

His fingers found moist feminine flesh, velvety soft and ready for him. Wet for him. He went mindless with need and without thinking, drew back and plunged between her legs.

The sheer shock of sensation bolted through him. She was hot and wet and ready. She cried out and wrapped her legs more firmly around him, rocking her hips forward to bring him deeper into her body.

It was at that exact moment that he realized he hadn't put on a condom.

"Summer, I forgot to put on—"

"I'm covered for birth control and have a clean bill of health. If you don't I'll kill you later, but for right now I just don't care. *Move*," she panted, arching against him, the command a guttural cry.

He did. "I'm healthy," he told her between thrusts.

"Wonderful," she breathed, clenching around him, her greedy feminine muscles holding him inside of her. "Let's work on that aim, why don't we."

He did, hitting the mark once more. Her keening cry and violent release triggered his own. He dug his toes into the mattress and pressed himself so far into her it was going to take a sonic blast to get him out. Breathing heavily, he collapsed on top of her, then rolled her onto his side. He was weak from release, utterly spent, and the happiness and contentment of the moment made him want to empty his heart and his head, tell her every sappy emotion that was running through his veins at the moment.

You're amazing. You're wonderful. You make me laugh. I love your smile. I don't want you to leave. Stay with me. Let's see where this is going. Let's take it to next level. I've never felt this way before and know I'll never feel this way again.

But he didn't. He merely kissed her. And when the candles had guttered in their holders and the fire was waning on the hearth, he still didn't have any idea how he was supposed to let her go. How he would ever stand back and let her slip out of his life.

But how could he ask her to stay? How could he ask her to give up her own life? It was too selfish. He knew he couldn't do that to her. Not when he didn't think he could make the sacrifice himself. He could never leave his home.

Could he?

8

THE NEXT MORNING dawned all too early for Summer.
She'd had to sneak back into her room and hurriedly
pack. She hadn't let herself think about what she was
doing, otherwise she wouldn't have been able to do it.

She didn't want to leave. She wanted to stay here with
him.

She wanted to listen to his laugh, feel his morning
scruff abrading her skin, thread her fingers through his
curly hair and tug his mouth to hers for a kiss. She could
feel him in every cell of her body, knew where he was
in relation to her without looking she was that aware of
him.

But…she had a home, a career and a family waiting
for her back in the States. The career was mobile, she
knew. She could just as easily take pictures here as she
could at home. She could visit her family. That was a
valid remedy, especially now that her mother seemed to
have turned a corner. And she could quite easily make
this her home. Hadn't she felt that connection from the
start? That sense of belonging on this particular soil?

Yes.

But…he hadn't asked her.

In fact, he hadn't brought up her leaving at all. To be fair, she hadn't given him a chance. She'd been so aware of time closing in on them she'd wanted to make the most of every minute. She'd mined his brain for his childhood memories, his likes and dislikes, his dreams, ambitions and goals. And then she'd made love to him over and over again.

She'd snuck away just before dawn and she'd never forget the way he looked, his bare leg swung out from beneath the blue velvet coverlet, the firelight playing over his auburn curls and ruddy skin, the way the shadows flickered over him, emphasizing his brawny, muscled frame. His face had been so relaxed in sleep, the hint of a smile still on his lips. Her heart had almost burst with emotion, looking at him. Because she was sneaky, she'd slipped her camera from her bag and taken a picture. The image was already indelibly burned onto her brain, but the photographer in her hadn't been able to resist.

Cam had been more subdued this morning when he'd been giving out the various prizes for their weekend. Her mother had won the Best Sleuth Award and Mimi had snagged Best Performer. Presently their bus had arrived and now their bags were being loaded. Mimi was talking to the couple from Dublin again and her mother had wandered toward the loch, a leather pouch in her hand.

She felt Cam move up beside her. "What's your mother doing?" he asked. His voice sounded odd. Rusty.

Tear pricked the back of her lids. "She's been sprinkling my father's ashes at special places along our journey," she explained. They watched her mother reach into the bag and lift her hand to the wind.

"Ah," he breathed and cleared his throat. "I'm honored."

"It'll be nice to know that he's here," she said. That made one of them, anyway. She sucked in a breath and dashed a tear from her cheek.

"Are you going to be all right, lass?" he asked.

She nodded. Made herself smile. "Yes."

People were boarding the bus and rather than linger, she leaned up and pressed a kiss to his cheek. "Thank you for a wonderful weekend. It's been…surreal."

"Summer—"

She hurried away before he could say more and took her seat on the coach. Momentarily, it took off. She determinedly didn't look at him. She couldn't bear it. She couldn't stand watching him fade out of her life.

Five minutes later, when she was certain that she was never going to be able to breathe properly again, a commotion at the back of the bus snagged her attention.

"Well, I never!"

"Do you see him?"

"What's he doing on that big black horse?"

Her head snapped up. Big, black horse? She hurried to the back of the bus and pressed her face against the glass.

Cam was riding for all he was worth, thundering along behind them like a Highland warrior. All that was missing was a claymore and a kilt.

"Stop," he shouted. "Stop the bus!"

Her heart threatening to burst out of her chest, Summer swung into action, darting to the front of the bus and begging the driver to stop.

By the time he opened the door and let her off, Cam

had come alongside the bus. He swung from the saddle and hurried toward her.

"I can't do it," he said. "I can't let you leave, not without telling you that I think that I'm in love with you. If it's not love, then I don't know what the hell it is, because it's damned powerful and it's because of you. I know it doesn't make sense, that we've only just met, but when you got on that bus it felt like you were taking a piece of me with you." He stepped closer and drew a half heart on her cheek. "We've got something special, lass. Tell me you feel it?"

She heard a collective "Aww" from behind her, followed by an "I knew it" from her mother.

Her eyes misted over. "You don't think we're being spectacularly stupid?"

He kissed her nose. "I'd rather be spectacularly stupid than forever regretting that I let you leave. Don't go," he whispered. "I know I'm being selfish, but if you're miserable here, I can give Little Cabbage Valley a try. But wherever we are on this earth, I think we're meant to be on it together."

Overjoyed, her heart ready to burst with happiness, she wrapped her arms around his neck and kissed him, then with a tilt of her head, gestured toward Harley. "The horse was a nice touch, but the truck would have been faster."

He smiled her favorite smile and inclined his head. "Maybe so, lass, but when we're telling this story to our grandchildren it's going to sound a whole lot better when we tell them that Grandpa rode up on a big black horse and whisked Granny back off to his castle instead of Grandpa chased the bus down in a beat-up Renault with a sticky clutch." He helped her onto the beast's back, then settled in behind her. "Don't you agree?"

She leaned back against him. "Another bull's-eye," she sighed.

Cam chuckled, the sound warm and familiar and so, so right. "Didn't I tell you I never miss the target?"

THE WAYFARER

1

When Isla Drummond planned her surprise trip to Scotland to visit the father she hadn't seen in four years, she'd imagined it going many different ways.

Finding him gone hadn't been one of them.

"Gone?" she repeated dully. "Gone where?"

"He's delivering a boat, ma'am, down Port Isaac way," the older gentleman told her.

Port Isaac? But that was in England, hundreds of miles from here. Oh, Lord. Isla looked around, taking in the boats in various stages of building and repair, the slight lapping of the waves against their hulls, and felt like crying. She'd never imagined that he wouldn't be here. Though she'd only visited her father twice before—both times before she'd hit her teens—whenever she thought of him, it was always at this place, in Lochawe, which was fittingly on Loch Awe, the longest freshwater loch in Scotland. Her father was a fourth-generation boat builder and by all accounts a master at his craft.

She should have checked in with him first, Isla thought, but the trip had been a spur of the moment one, completely unplanned, and she'd decided to surprise him. She grimaced.

So much for that.

"Do you have any idea when he'll be back?" Isla asked. She was only here for a few days, hadn't been able to arrange pet care for any longer—she fostered animals from the local rescue shelter, not to mention her own—especially on such short notice. Honestly, had her mother not joined Harry—the man she secretly prayed her mother would marry—on that Alaskan cruise, she wouldn't have thought to make the impromptu travel arrangements.

But it had been years since she'd spent time with her father, having last seen him at her college graduation, and she'd missed him. Because her mother blamed her father's love of country for the demise of their short-lived marriage, she'd made it difficult for Isla as a child. As an adult, Isla was determined to change that and that conviction had been made even stronger the minute she'd stepped off the plane in Glasgow.

She could *breathe* here, felt a connection to the earth that simply surpassed understanding.

"I'm not sure, lass," the man told her. "I think Alec talked to him last," he said, shooting a look at the office. "Let me fetch him for you and maybe he can help you out."

Alec? She recognized the name. Her father often spoke fondly of him. Alec was doing this or Alec was working on that, Alec was meeting him at the pub.

"Oy, Alec!" the older man hollered over his shoulder. "Could you come here a minute? There's a young lady here looking for Fergus."

Because all the men she'd seen working at the boat

yard thus far were either older, like her father, or teenagers, she just assumed that the mysterious Alec would be one or the other, too.

Wrong again.

The frowning man who walked into view was a tall thirty-something, broad-shouldered Scottish Adonis with muscles on top of muscles and a pair of pale gray eyes that were curiously bright and warm, a compelling combination. His hair was the color of dark coffee, a bit curly and endearingly unkempt. He wore a faded red T-shirt that had seen better days, a blue flannel shirt knotted around his waist and a pair of jeans that didn't so much mold his frame as caress it.

Though the wind didn't stir, Isla felt a hot tornado start at her feet and whirl upward, singeing her nerve endings and leaving her curiously, disconcertingly breathless. She could feel the blood moving sluggishly through her body despite the fact that her heart was galloping in her chest, thundering in her ears. Her mouth went bone dry, forcing her to swallow.

He was wiping his hands on a towel and faltered a bit when he saw her. She watched recognition flash in his gaze a moment before he reached her, but beyond that his face remained neutral—purposely so, she suspected.

"This young lady wants to know when Fergus will be back," the older gentleman explained.

Alec's cautious gaze swung to hers once more and he extended his hand. "Alec MacKinnon," he said, evidently trying to force an identity out of her—merely for confirmation purposes, she was sure. For whatever reason, she knew that he knew exactly who she was.

"Isla Drummond," she said, taking the proffered

palm. A current slid up her arm at the brief contact. His hand was exceptionally warm and strong, callused from his trade. She repressed a shiver, dimly wondering what the hell was wrong with her. He was a man, that was all. Granted an extremely good-looking man, but her reaction to him was simply off the hook. Ridiculous.

The older man's brushy brows winged up his forehead and he gasped, seemingly astonished. "Isla? *You're* Isla?" His excited gaze instantly swung to Alec. "You've got to get in touch with Fergus! He'll be sick if he misses her!" He looked back at Isla, a grizzled grin still on his face, his brown eyes twinkling. "It's a pleasure to meet you, lass. I've heard a lot about you. I'm Donnell, by the way," he said with a nod. "Donnell McLeod."

Pleased with her reception from him at least, Isla returned his grin. "The pleasure's mine, Mr. McLeod. Thank you."

She turned back to Alec, her body still vibrating strangely. "Do you have any idea when my father will be back?"

The color of the water beyond him, those intriguing eyes studied her more carefully than she liked. "He's supposed to deliver the boat this afternoon. Last time I talked to him he planned to spend the night and then start making his way back up." He winced. "It's around a ten-hour drive, so I expect he'll be in sometime late tomorrow night." He paused. "How long are you here for?"

"Just a few days," she said. But if he got in tomorrow night, then at least this trip wouldn't have been for nothing. She'd have a little time with him at least. A thought struck. "Does he have a mobile phone now?"

A ghost of a smile hovered on Alec's lips and somehow that little expression seemed more potent than a full-fledged grin. "Afraid not. He doesn't care for technology."

She gave a mental eye roll. Didn't she know that? She'd lobbied hard for the computer so that they could communicate via email and instant messaging, but her father still didn't particularly care for it, despite the convenience. In fact the only technological advances he seemed enamored of were high definition television and the DVR. The thought made her smile.

"Right," she said, nodding. "I should have known. Do you think he'll check in again?"

"I don't expect him to, but I'll ring and leave a message at his destination for him to call when he gets there. I'll make sure they know that it's urgent." Another pause, then a slight wince. "I take it he didn't know you were coming? He wouldn't have offered to make such a lengthy delivery if he'd known."

Feeling more than a little stupid, she grimaced. "It was a spur of the moment trip," she said. "I wanted to surprise him."

"I wish you could have," Alec told her. "He would have been thrilled."

Though there was no censure in his tone whatsoever, she felt it all the same.

"Where are you staying, lass?" Mr. McLeod wanted to know.

Actually, she'd planned on staying with her dad, but since he wasn't here other arrangements would have to be made. She'd passed a bed and breakfast on the way in and decided it would have to do. "Nowhere, yet," she admitted. She looked over her shoulder. "I'll check out the local—"

"I'm sure your father would want you to stay at his place," Alec told her. "I'll give you my key."

He had a key to her father's place? *He* had a key and *she* didn't? It shouldn't annoy her—it was unreasonable considering this was only the third time in her entire life that she'd visited—and yet…it did. Who was he, anyway, to have a key to her father's place?

"I don't mind staying at the B&B," she said.

"Your father wouldn't hear of it," Mr. McLeod insisted. He jerked his head toward the cottage on the hill. "Take her up there, Alec, and help her get settled. Fergus wouldn't want it any other way."

She imagined not, but the idea of going anywhere with Alec made her simultaneously keen with anticipation and sick with dread. It was ridiculous how much the man affected her and they'd only been breathing the same air for a few minutes. He made her achy and prickly—not a good combination.

After the briefest hesitation, Alec nodded. "Just let me go make that call first and then we'll go," he said.

Though it would feel strange staying at her father's place without him there, Isla had to admit that she'd rather do that than stay at a B&B. You could tell a lot about a person by their space and, while she had no intention of snooping, she was curious about what sort of books he liked to read, what snacks he kept in the fridge. Things that she'd have known if she'd grown up with him, if he'd been more a part of her life. As it was, he seemed more like a benevolent uncle than a real dad.

When she'd been a child, she'd blamed him for that, but as an adult she could see things weren't so cut and dried. Though there was still some residual hurt—she used to dream that he'd simply show up one day, and tell her that he was moving to the States because he couldn't stand to be away from her—she'd nevertheless matured enough to realize that *this* was his home and things would have never worked out with her mother anyway.

Sad? Yes. But equally true.

Theirs had been an ill-fated match from the beginning and she was the only evidence that it had ever existed to start with. Interestingly neither of her parents had ever remarried—though hopefully her mother was close now—and she wasn't quite sure what to make of that. Had their relationship left such a bad taste in the other's mouth that they hadn't wanted to try again? Or had they simply never found another? From what she'd observed of her mother, she'd simply been too…bitter to let anything remotely resembling love in, she'd treated Isla more like a trophy than a child, one she'd resented as much as loved.

It hadn't been easy being Lisa Drummond's daughter, that was for sure.

Alec strolled out once more, the afternoon sun gilding his dark locks with a touch of burnished gold. Her breath got stuck in her throat and fire licked through her veins, inciting the urge to fidget.

"Okay," he said. "I've left word for him to ring my mobile, so I'll be sure I won't miss him."

"Thank you," she said, feeling suddenly ridiculous. "I know I should have called, but I—" She shrugged helplessly. "I thought a surprise would be nicer."

"It's still going to be a surprise," Alec told her. He nodded toward her rental. "This yours?"

"For the duration, yes."

He nodded, his face still irritatingly expressionless. "Follow me, then."

2

ALEC MACKINNON HAD never walked into a brick wall, but after laying eyes on Isla Drummond he imagined he knew what it felt like.

When Donnell had summoned him from the office, he'd been distracted thinking of the plans for the new skiff he had in mind, and hadn't been expecting a pretty girl, much less one that made him feel like an invisible barrier had suddenly been erected in front of him, knocking him just as breathless as stupid.

Alec wasn't accustomed to either.

In fact, he had more practice causing the effect than experiencing it and, not surprisingly, he preferred the former.

And if seeing her had snatched the wind from his sails, then realizing that she was Fergus's daughter was enough to capsize him altogether. Though he hadn't seen any recent pictures of her, he could have picked her out of a crowd with little to no effort at all. Isla Drummond was the feminine version of her father—same curly red hair, same bright blue eyes ringed in a darker hue. She reminded him of one of those Victorian dolls his mother collected. Smooth skin, a perfect oval face and a sweetness there, for lack of a better term, that instantly struck a chord.

But there was nothing sweet in the way he'd reacted to her, that was for damned sure.

To *Fergus's* daughter.

He supposed the hard-on would make it easier for his mentor to unman him. He stifled a dark laugh. A bigger target, after all.

Bloody hell.

Of all the women in the world for him to be so viciously attracted to, why in the hell did it have to be *that* one? Alec thought with furious despair.

Especially since, given what he knew of her—which was precious damned little, he'd admit—he didn't particularly like her. How could he, when he'd seen his friend silently suffer for years? Though Fergus had never had anything but glowing things to say about his daughter, Alec had always wondered why she never came around. Fergus had been to Georgia a couple of times to see her since Alec had started his apprenticeship with him some ten years ago, but to his knowledge this was her first appearance in Scotland.

And it had been unplanned and unannounced.

Bizarre.

Working strictly with what he'd seen over the years, he'd imagined Fergus's daughter as being a spoiled little brat with no regard for anyone but herself. He'd watched her father put in twice as many hours as men half his age in order to send money to the States to finance her college education and other than the occasional telephone call or email—which Fergus never failed to report—she seemed to have precious little time for him. He'd already been irritated on behalf of his friend—his mentor—and the fact that she'd arrived without notice, without even having the courtesy to tell her father she was coming, only angered him more.

What? Was Fergus supposed to drop everything because she'd finally decided she should come visit her father? Was he supposed to rearrange his schedule at her whim? Her convenience? Alec's gaze slid to his rearview mirror, where he watched her carefully pull in behind him.

Evidently so.

And the really terrible truth of it was…Fergus *would* drop everything. Unfortunately, he wasn't in a place where he could do it easily and so no doubt the old man would push himself to the brink to make the drive back so that he could see her before she left.

In a few days.

Another puzzle. Why come halfway around the world if you only had a few days? What was so pressing that she had to return so quickly? Frankly, he didn't think it was her job. From what little Fergus had said, Isla made costume jewelry out of semi-precious stones, old bits of crockery, or anything else that struck her fancy. Undoubtedly she worked, but he would imagine that her schedule was flexible. He was presuming a lot, he knew, but as far as he was concerned she'd given him permission to speculate when she'd shown up without warning.

A big ball of dread in his belly, an unmatched sense of anticipation tightening his fingers, he drove his truck to the top of the hill and pulled into Fergus's driveway. Burning the clutch out behind him, she whined up the hill as well and stuttered to a stop next to him.

That poor car, he thought, his lips twitching as she pushed the hair out of her face and clambered with more dignity than he would have imagined from behind the wheel.

"Not used to a standard?" he asked, quirking a brow.

"What tipped you off?" she deadpanned. "The gravel I slung when I pulled out of the parking lot or the beautiful way I rode the clutch *and* the accelerator as I nursed it up the hill? It was all they had. Another disadvantage to not planning," she muttered under her breath. She reached into the backseat and pulled out a wheeled bag unlike any he'd ever seen. It was covered in cats—tabbies, Persians, black, white and calico, some of them kittens, some full grown.

Belatedly remembering his manners, he hurried over and took it from her. "Guess that's easy enough to find on the luggage carousel," he said, gesturing to the bag.

She grinned and the simple rearrangement of her rosy lips made his chest constrict and his dick twitch. "I haven't missed it yet."

"So you're one of those then? A cat person?"

She nodded and followed him through the gate. "And a dog person and a bird person. Basically anything with fur and feathers."

"No scales?"

She gave a shudder. "Definitely no scales. Just keeping the dogs away from the cats and the cats away from the birds is a challenge. Adding something with scales into the mix is out of the question."

He pulled his keys from his pocket, located the right

one, then inserted it into the lock and opened the door.
A loud "meow" instantly greeted them.

"Oh," she cried delightedly. "This must be Ahab."
She dropped down and ran a hand over the tabby cat's
enormous head, resulting in a loud purr.

"Since you'll be staying here, you won't mind feeding
him, I hope," Alec told her. "It'll save me a trip."

She stood, scooping the overweight cat up in her
arms. The purring increased and Ahab went boneless
in her arms, lapping up her attention.

"You take care of him when my dad travels, then?"

"On the very rare occasion he leaves home, yes. It's
easy enough," he told her. "I live next door."

She fumbled, almost dropping Ahab, and the cat
yowled in protest. Color flooding her cheeks, she
kneeled once more and put him down. "Next door?" she
repeated. "Really?" she added less enthusiastically.

For whatever reason her response made him want to
laugh. So she wasn't any more enamored of him than
he was of her? he wondered. Now that was interesting
and certainly not a response he was accustomed to. His
opinion of her had been formed based on years of what
he perceived as neglect of her father. Hers had been
formed more quickly—as in the last ten minutes—and
he couldn't help but wonder what exactly it was about
him that had put her off.

He shouldn't care…and yet he did.

Not good.

He'd never been able to resist a puzzle or a challenge
and Isla Drummond was quickly becoming both.

She looked around, seemingly absorbing every detail of the room, and there was a wistfulness about her

expression—a longing—that made him feel acutely uncomfortable.

"I should go," he said, jerking his finger toward the door. "Leave you to get settled."

Though he'd always felt right at home in Fergus's cottage, he felt like he was intruding here, witnessing something he had no right to see.

She looked up then, her blue eyes a little brighter than they'd been only seconds before. "Of course. Thank you for escorting me."

He took the key off the ring and handed it to her, and the brush of her skin against his felt significant, intimate even.

"I'm just down the hill if you need anything," he said. He owed it to Fergus to be courteous, didn't he? No ulterior motive. Nothing special about her, he told himself. Just because she suddenly looked lost and lonelier than he'd ever seen a person didn't mean that she was affecting him differently than any other woman in the same situation would, right?

Hell, he was human. It was obvious that something was wrong and he was a man who liked to fix things, who'd never been good at walking away. He'd never passed a stranded motorist and was the go-to guy when any of his friends had needed to move. He should leave—definitely needed to go—and yet...

"Listen, Isla—"

"I'll be fine," she insisted. "I'm a little tired actually. It was a long flight and a long drive, particularly for someone who doesn't know how to drive a stick-shift and isn't accustomed to driving on the wrong side of the car and the wrong side of the road. And those roundabouts? I prefer a good old-fashioned stop light and traditional intersection," she said, laughing softly at herself.

Honestly, he'd been so wrapped up in the fact that she'd arrived without warning that he hadn't stopped to consider how much courage it had taken to come here—to fly over, then get behind the wheel and drive for nearly two hours on unfamiliar roads, in an even more unfamiliar car.

He considered her again, truly looked at her, and decided she had more pluck than he'd given her credit for.

He admired pluck.

"Roundabouts are easy enough once you get used to them," he said. "Traffic moves more swiftly."

"Yes," she said, her eyes widening in outrage. "Because no one stops. You just keep circling around until you find your exit and sling-shot off of it like a pin-ball being ejected from a game."

He chuckled at her description, glad that she didn't seem quite so gloomy anymore. "I'll come up when I hear from Fergus," he said, making his way to the door once more.

"Would you have him call me here?" she asked. "I'm going to stay in until I hear from him."

He nodded, then took his leave. Once outside, Alec took a deep cleansing breath, hoping to clear his head, but then swore softly under his breath.

He instinctively knew the head on his shoulders wasn't the one that was going to give him trouble. The one south of his zipper was going to be a bloody bugger, that was for damned sure.

Time to sail, Alec thought. He always thought better on the water.

3

THE QUIET CLOSE of the door punctuated Isla's sigh and she hung her head and took a deep breath.

Coming hadn't been a mistake, she told herself. She was glad she was here, even if things hadn't gone according to plan. So she hadn't run across the parking lot à la Julie Andrews *The Sound of Music*–style straight into her father's open arms? She was still here and, barring any unforeseen complications, would see him shortly. In the meantime she planned to familiarize herself with his house—his things—and spend a little time wandering the village.

Also, she hadn't been lying when she'd told Alec—thinking about him immediately made her shiver—that she was tired. She wasn't a stranger to flying, but twelve hours in the air, not to mention the layovers and the two-hour drive here, had certainly knocked the wind out of her sails. In fact, she suspected adrenaline had had more to do with her energy the last few hours and now that she'd burned all that up—not to mention copious amounts of caffeine—she was quite exhausted.

Since it had been more than fifteen years since her

last visit, Isla had expected things to look different at her father's house.

They didn't.

The stone fireplace and plaster walls were the same and, though her dad had bought a new sofa and television, those items were in the same position she remembered. Various sailing prints covered the walls and a stack of drafting paper, along with a pencil, was sitting neatly on the kitchen table. His teakettle was the same— a heavy cast iron affair—and she recognized what he'd told her was his mother's tea set on the small kitchen counter. Seeing it brought a pang.

She'd only met her grandmother a couple of times and remembered a plump, happy woman with kind eyes and a sweet smile. Her grandmother had left her a cameo brooch when she'd passed away and Isla had made it into a necklace, one that was always around her neck.

A washer and dryer were tucked beneath the kitchen cabinets—those would come in handy, she thought— and a large wooden clothes dryer was suspended from the ceiling. She'd remembered being completely enamored with that as a child, wanting to do laundry just so she could hang her wet things over it and then hoist it up and out of the way.

After taking a peek in the fridge and discovering her father had little more than milk and refrigerated cookie dough, she moved on to inspect the rest of the house. Her father's room was just as she remembered it, with a big iron bed and stack of books on the nightstand. Seeing his shoes lined up like little soldiers at the foot of his bed made a lump well in her throat. Ridiculous. They were only shoes and yet… Like everything else in this house, they'd been placed there with great care.

She wouldn't call her father fastidious, but careful and attentive certainly came to mind.

The bathroom was just as tidy. Toothbrush and shaving accessories properly stowed, a bottle of lotion and hand soap next to the sink. Because she couldn't resist, she opened the medicine cabinet and found only a few herbal supplements and a jar of anti-wrinkle cream. She smiled and shook her head.

The only area left was what had been her room, and looking in there was something she actually dreaded. When she'd lived here as a girl, her father had painted the walls pink for her and outfitted a white twin-size bed with a coverlet covered in butterflies. It had been whimsical and girlie and, though her mother had tried to recreate the look, it had never felt the same. Possibly because imagining her big, burly weather-beaten father selecting those things for her had been what made it so special. Like everything else he did in his life, he'd done it with thought and deliberation, and that's what had made it perfect.

She'd avoided even looking in the direction of her bedroom when she'd entered the hall because she'd been afraid of what she might find. Had he redecorated because she hadn't come back? Had he decided to make it a proper guest room and get rid of the frilly curtains and unicorn prints? The pale yellow braided rug?

She couldn't blame him if he had. She hadn't been here in more than fifteen years. He was perfectly within his rights to have made it an office or guest room. Hell, he could have put a hot tub in here and that would have been perfectly reasonable. She knew all of this, of course. Even believed it. But a part of her desperately wanted the room to be the same, to be just as she'd left it, with her hair barrettes and Nancy Drew books still on the nightstand.

Unreasonable?

Without a doubt. And yet…

Isla took a deep breath and nudged the door open. A sob caught in her throat and she covered her mouth, felt tears prick the backs of her lids.

It was the same—absolutely the same—and seeing this room and knowing that he'd kept it as it was for her meant more than she would have ever dreamed. Equally weary, joyful and relieved, she made the short trek to the bed, lay down and curled up on her side.

It felt so good to be home, she thought.

IT WAS SEVERAL HOURS later before his cell rang and Alec knew without looking who it would be. He tied the boat off and answered the phone.

"Alec," Fergus said, worry in his voice. "They told me to call, that it was urgent. Is everything okay?"

"Everything's fine, Fergus," he assured him. "I just wanted to make sure that you called before you came back because we've got a bit of news for you." He felt terrible basically ruining Isla's surprise and it belatedly occurred to him that he should have left his cell with her so that she could have answered this call.

"News?" his old friend repeated. "Happy news or I'm gonna need a pint news?"

"Both actually," Alec told him, smiling. "We had a visitor today," he said.

"I don't know what's newsworthy about that," he said. "We get visitors all the time."

It was true. Lochawe was a pretty little town with a decent amount of tourist action and occasionally, intrigued by the boats—or looking for boat rentals—people would drop in.

"We do," he admitted. "But they're usually not your daughter."

A profound silence echoed across the line then, "Isla? My Isla is there?"

The astonishment, the ache and longing in Fergus's voice was palpable. "She is. She meant to surprise you," he told him. He turned toward the water and looked out across the loch. "Said it was a spur of the minute trip and had decided not to call."

"Well, it's definitely a surprise," he said. "I just talked to her last week and she didn't mention a thing about a visit, just talked about a new cat she was fostering, a line of jewelry she was working on. She didn't say— She never mentioned—" He swore. "Something must have happened," he said. "She must need me and I'm here. Did she say how long she was staying?"

Dammit, this was a conversation Fergus should be having with her, not him. He winced, tried to sound matter of fact. "Just a few days."

Fergus sighed. "I figured as much. She's not going to leave those animals for long," he said, a smile in his voice.

"Animals?"

"She's got a houseful," Fergus told him. "She works with the local shelter there in Dahlia Grove and takes the animals that are next up on the chopping block, as it were, until a home can be found for them. Sometimes she gets the ones that are too sick to be in the shelter, who need some rehabilitation before being put up for adoption. She's got a tender heart, my Isla. She always has. Since she works from home, she says it's ideal."

So that's what she'd meant by anything with "fur and feathers." And if she had as many pets as Fergus seemed to think, then finding someone to care for them for more than a few days couldn't have been easy. Hell, he only had one animal—Mackie, his Portuguese Water dog—and on the rare occasions he traveled somewhere that he couldn't take him, he typically ended up leaving him with one of his siblings. More often than not, Cam, who had a sprawling estate with lots of room and water for Mackie to play in.

"I can't believe she's there," Fergus said, wonder in his voice. "I've been waiting for…" He couldn't finish.

"You'll be back soon enough," Alec told him. "You've delivered the boat, made good time. With an empty trailer you'll make better on the way home."

"One can hope," Fergus said. "The truck is running hot. I was going to get it checked out before I started back, but—"

"Don't," Alec told him. "It should keep until you get home. Just come on back. You'll drive yourself crazy if you don't."

"How does she look, my girl?" Fergus wanted to know.

Alec chuckled. "She looks like you but, no offense, is a damned sight prettier."

Fergus laughed. "No offense taken, lad. I know what you mean. I've always thought she looked like me, but was afraid that was vanity speaking. It's good to hear that someone else sees the resemblance. Did you take her up to the house? I don't want her staying at a B&B."

"I did," he confirmed. "About three hours ago. She was tired. I imagine she took a nap, but she asked me to have you call the house, said she wouldn't leave until she heard from you. You need a cell phone, old man," Alec ribbed him. "She could have called you herself."

"You'll look after her until I get there?" Fergus asked.

Look after her? He thought he already had. He'd given her a key to the house and taken her up there. What else was there to do?

Besides, given the way the blood left his brain and camped in his groin, he was the last damned person who needed to be "looking after" Fergus's daughter. "Er…"

"Alec, you can't leave her on her own. She hasn't been to visit since she was a wee lass, since she was eleven. Her mother— Nevermind," he went on. "You have to show her some hospitality and you can start by taking her to dinner tonight. You'd leave her to break bread alone? My daughter?"

Alec suppressed a long sigh. "Of course not, Fergus."

His old friend released a grateful breath. "Excellent. There's nothing too pressing at the shop that can't wait until I get back. Leave the other men to it and you look after my girl. Take her out to Lock Etive, to Kilchurn castle and over to Glenashdale Falls and the Giants' Graves."

Excellent. He was going to be a bloody tour guide. "Fergus—"

"Alec, I know I'm imposing, that I'm asking a lot." He paused. "But this is the first time Isla has been back on Scottish soil in years and I want her to see some of it, to breathe it in. It's her heritage. Just show her a little of it for me, please. I'll take over as soon as I get in. I'll start back now. I—"

"Fergus, you need to rest for the night before you tackle the drive back and you know it. It's late. What good is it going to do you if you wear yourself out to get here? Rest up tonight and head out first thing in the morning. You can be here by late afternoon tomorrow. Even if you drive the whole way home tonight, you'll just end up sleeping all day when you get here."

A thoughtful pause, then, "I suppose you're right."

Alec grinned. "I usually am."

"Codswallop," the older man muttered gruffly. "You'll see to my girl? You'll take care of her? Make sure she enjoys herself until I get there? Maybe take her out on the boat?"

Alec winced and rubbed the bridge of his nose, knowing that, for reasons he couldn't explain, he was agreeing to his own ruination. "Of course."

"Thank you, Alec," Fergus said, his voice rife with relief. "You're a good lad."

A doomed, stupid lad more like, Alec thought, but what was the point in arguing?

It was a damned good thing he was better at saying no to his father, Alec thought, otherwise he would find himself the CEO of MacKinnon Holdings.

And really, given the choice between being Isla's tour guide or CEO of the family company—a position he thought his sister should have—he'd take Isla any day.

Even though taking her was exactly what he feared.

4

BECAUSE HER FATHER had told her when he'd called earlier that Alec would be taking her to dinner tonight, she wasn't surprised when he knocked on the door.

What was surprising was that, even though she was convinced that he couldn't be any better looking than he'd been when she'd seen him at the boat shop earlier, he was.

Despite the fact that it was June and the days were typically pretty, the evening had cooled down considerably. Alec had dressed accordingly in a dark gray wool cable knit sweater, another pair of worn jeans and brown leather boots. His dark hair was still a little wet on the ends, evidence of his recent shower, and he'd taken a razor to his face and removed the five o'clock stubble she'd noticed earlier. All in all he looked like he'd just stepped off the cover of a magazine—or a cologne ad; the scent wafting to her as he hesitated in the doorway was something slightly musky with a salty finish.

And her father had charged him with baby-sitting her.

How humiliating.

How thrilling.

Pasting a smile onto her face, she stepped back to let him in. "You don't have to do this, you know," she felt obliged to point out. "I'm a big girl. I can find my way down to the pub."

His stormy gray gaze did a slow sweep over her body, gratifyingly lingering in all the right places and then found her face. "I'm sure you can, but you aren't going to. As much for my own pleasure as a public service, I can't let you get back behind the wheel of that vehicle."

She chuckled. "I made it here, didn't I?"

"You did," he said, nodding. "But at whose peril, I wonder?" he asked with mock concern.

She laughed again, glad that he seemed to be less reserved than he was earlier in the day. Was it because he'd talked to her father? Because her father had told him to show her a good time? She knew he had because the well-meaning interferer had told her that when he'd called. "Don't worry," he'd said. "Alec is going to entertain you until I get home."

Oh, goody.

A pity project. And yet she had to admit she was secretly a bit excited about it. After all, what girl wouldn't want to be hauled around a romantic country by a hot Scot? Hell, she'd happily let him drive. Besides, while she wasn't in the market for romance—her heart had taken a beating the last go round, thank you very much— a little harmless flirtation could do wonders for her ego. It was only temporary after all. A strange pang struck at the thought, startling her, but she determinedly ignored it.

According to her dad, he expected to be here sometime late tomorrow afternoon. He'd been so disappointed that she'd missed him and had assured her that he'd hurry. He had so many things he'd wanted to show her, he'd said, and had sounded more excited than she could ever recall.

It made her sad that she'd waited so long to visit, that she'd let not rocking the boat with her mother snatch away so much time with her dad. It had been wrong, she realized now. She should have revolted sooner. Did she appreciate her mother? Of course. But simply going along with her to avoid conflict had hurt both herself and her father. When her mom returned from cruise she was going to be in for quite a shock, one that she might as well get used to.

Starting now, Isla had every intention of spending more time in Scotland, more time with her dad. Come to think of it, she might see about spending Christmas here with him. Other than the first two of her life— which she couldn't remember, of course—she'd never done that. Finding pet care that time of year wouldn't be easy, but maybe between now and then she could work something out. Her neighbor seemed to be interested in fostering. Maybe she could bring her on board in time for the holidays.

"So you talked to your dad?" he asked.

"I did," she told him. "And much as I appreciate you going to dinner because I hate to eat alone, you seriously don't have to accompany me to every old ruin and bit of loch my dad wants me to see. He did mention that you might take me sailing and I admit I'd love to do that. I love the water and here it is…simply beautiful," she finished, knowing the description was inadequate.

"I don't mind," he said, almost convincingly. He must

really care for her father, she decided. "And I'd be happy to take you sailing. I go out every day. It's my therapy," he explained.

She smiled. "I could use a bit of that." And that was as good a description as she'd ever heard for the peace that came over her when she was near a lake or stream or the ocean. She'd always thought it was because her father loved it so, that she'd inherited the proclivity from him.

"Shall we go?" he asked. "I'd guess you're starving. Your dad eats most meals in the pub and, in my experience, keeps very little in the house."

She understood that. Cooking for one wasn't something she enjoyed and eating alone was particularly miserable. Whereas her dad ate at the local pub, she either ordered in or went down to a little sports bar near her house. Something about the noise and the atmosphere made her feel less alone. It was funny, really. She didn't mind living alone, enjoyed having sole control of the remote and the entire bed. She preferred not being accountable to anyone, to owning every minute of her time and spending it in the way she saw fit, but she hated to eat by herself. Meals were meant to be shared, in her opinion. Conversation never failed to make a dish taste better.

When she and Mark had parted ways she'd been more upset over the lack of a dinner companion than the actual demise of the relationship. Interestingly, though she'd liked him well enough, she'd never imagined a permanent life with him, his and her towels and the whole shared cohabitation bit. She hadn't imagined that with anyone, come to think, and briefly wondered if, like her parents, she was more inclined to liking her own company.

For whatever reason, the thought made her sad. Her gaze slid to Alec, who was waiting patiently for her, and she felt an odd tug behind her navel, a curious pull that startled the breath out of her.

Or maybe she'd just never met the right person.

Maybe she'd been on the wrong continent.

Frightening though the possibility was, she'd admit it was preferable to the other thought.

IF HE'D HOPED THAT his attraction would have lessened or that she would have miraculously been transformed into a soulless hag since the last time he saw her, then those hopes definitely had been in vain, Alec thought as he held the door open to the pub for Isla.

She'd showered and smelled like a ripe peach, fruity and mellow. Mouthwatering. Heat stirred in his loins, once again making him grit his teeth. She wore a dark green sweater that hugged her well-proportioned frame and a pair of boot-cut jeans that clung to an equally mouthwatering ass. A rather large cameo dangled between her breasts and earrings made from bits of smashed-up china hung from her ears. She was effortlessly beautiful and had she been anyone but Fergus's daughter, he would have made a play for her quicker than you could say "kilt."

But she *was* Fergus's daughter, he reminded himself, and therefore completely off-limits, sexually speaking.

He gloomily suspected the next twenty-four hours were going to be hell.

"A pint, please, Malcolm," he said, signaling the pub

owner. "And a menu." He pulled a chair back for Isla. "What would you like to drink?"

"Whatever you're having," she demurred.

He ordered a pint for Isla as well and smothered a smile as the aging pub owner walked over with their drinks to inspect his newest customer. "Well, as I live and breathe," he said in a wondering tone. "You're a Drummond if I ever saw one. You'd be Fergus's girl, wouldn't you?"

Seemingly pleased that she'd been so easily recognized, she smiled up at him. "I would be. Isla Drummond," she said, extending her small hand.

"Malcolm Campbell," he told her. "And that pint and whatever you're having is on the house." He looked at Alec and frowned. "Not yours, mind. I see your sorry face around here all the time. So much so that I ought to charge you extra for having to look at it so often."

A low throaty laugh bubbled up Isla's throat as Malcolm went back to the bar, and her eyes crinkled delightfully in the corners as she smiled at Alec. "You're a regular, are you?"

He didn't like to eat alone, so yes. He nodded. "I'm down here at least five nights out of seven."

She took a sip of her drink and he watched her eyes widen appreciatively. They should. That was an organic brew, one of Scotland's best. "What do you do the other two?"

"Starve," he deadpanned.

Another soft laugh, then she picked up the menu and gave it a quick once over. "Anything particular you'd recommend?"

"Despite fancying himself a stand-up comic, Malcolm is an excellent cook. Everything is good, but if you're looking for traditional Scottish fare, then I would suggest the fish and chips. It doesn't get much better than that."

She closed her menu. "Then fish and chips it is." He shouted their order to Malcolm, then settled and tried to think of an appropriate conversation starter, when what he'd really like to ask was "what the hell are you doing here?"

She cast an expectant glance around the pub and seemed to relax more fully into her chair.

Were he permitted to flirt, he'd have lots of things to say to her, but as he wasn't, he found himself annoyingly tongue-tied. "So you're a jewelry designer?" he blurted out, for lack of anything better.

Looking a bit startled at the abrupt change in subject, she swallowed the bit of ale in her mouth and nodded in affirmation. "I am," she said. "I started beading in grade school and things sort of morphed from there."

"I'm assuming you made the earrings?"

She fingered one. "I did. I actually got the idea from a friend years ago. She dropped one of her great-grandmother's teacups and was so distraught I wanted to help, to do something with it to preserve the china. I made an entire set—earrings, pendant and a ring out of it and gave it to her for her birthday." She shrugged. "Word got out and since then I've repurposed hundreds of different things into jewelry. I've got a website as well and sell my stuff into lots of high-end boutiques around the south. It took a while, but business is good."

He had to admire her creativity and he liked the idea of things not being lost, being repurposed, as she'd said. He'd done the same with various parts from boats. From bits of hardware to the actual wood, nothing was ever truly beyond saving.

"And you work from home? That's what gives you the time to foster animals?"

Her eyes widened significantly. "Looks like Dad's been chatty," she said, taking another pull from her glass.

"Not chatty," he told her. "He mentioned it when I told him that you'd only be here for a few days, said you'd have to get back to your animals."

A soft smile played over her mouth. "I started volunteering at our shelter when I was in high school and decided to foster when I graduated from college and got my own place." A faraway look darkened her gaze. "I couldn't stand the thought of the animals being put down—I saw so many that were good pets, but just… unwanted. It's easy to make a donation," she explained. "And I'm thankful that so many people do, but—" she lifted her shoulders in small shrug "—I wanted to do more, to get in there and get my hands dirty, to make a difference."

He nodded, once again suitably impressed. Talk was cheap and Isla Drummond, much like her father, wasn't a talker.

She grinned again and cocked her head endearingly. "As a result I've got two dogs, two cats and four birds that are my own, and right now I'm fostering a pit bull that had been left for dead after a fight, a pair of flea-bitten malnourished kittens and a lop-eared rabbit who likes to chew through my electrical cords." She paused thoughtfully. "I'll probably keep the kittens," she said. "They'll keep my older cats young."

Malcolm delivered their plates, then nodded and took up his post again behind the bar.

"And the pit bull and the rabbit?" he asked, genuinely astonished and intrigued.

She winced. "Unfortunately, even though the pit is a sweet-natured dog, he's got the taste of blood in his mouth and I'm afraid he'd go after one of my other dogs. He's going to have to go to a home where there aren't any other pets. It's a shame," she said. "Dog-fighting is such a terrible, terrible thing."

He agreed. Pits were beautiful animals and the morons who fought them, aside from it being cruel and inhumane, ultimately ruined the dogs. "And the rabbit?" he asked.

"I'll find a home for her."

"So who is taking care of your menagerie while you're gone?"

"A fellow friend from the shelter—Rex."

Because anything resembling good sense had evaporated the minute he clapped eyes on her, he automatically disliked Rex, simply because he was a man.

Alec drained what was left of his drink and called for another. What the hell, he thought.

If he was going to be stupid, he might as well have an excuse and in his cups was just as good as any.

5

ISLA DIDN'T KNOW if it was the company or the place—probably a combination of both—but this meal was the best she'd ever had. And the ale… It tasted good against her tongue and went down smooth. The pleasant warmth it sent winding through her limbs was going to get her in trouble if she didn't back off a bit. That warmth, which was rapidly dismantling her inhibitions, in addition to the fire of attraction burning in her blood, was a very dangerous combination.

And gratifyingly, not just for her.

Though he'd been a bit standoffish and careful when he'd first shown up at her door tonight, Alec was anything but now. That gorgeous gray gaze sparkled with enough interest to make her nipples pebble behind her bra and the occasional lingering look, as though he didn't quite know what to make of her but was interested in learning more, made her stomach go all warm and squishy. He wasn't overtly flirting—seemed to be trying not to, actually, no doubt out of respect for her father—but he was definitely, *definitely* attracted to her.

She tried not to look too pleased with herself. But,

oh man, how she wanted him. Had she been sexually attracted to a guy before? Certainly. But never like this, never so keenly aware, so into one. She kept imagining licking the side of his neck and pushing her hands into his hair. Her belly gave another clench.

Time to lay off the alcohol, Isla decided, otherwise…

Otherwise she might just do exactly what she wanted—*him*.

And that, for reasons she couldn't ferret out of her foggy brain at the moment, was a bad idea.

"Have you always lived in Lochawe?" Isla asked him, deciding that she'd shared enough personal history.

He shook his head, chased a bead of sweat down his glass with his thumb and a small smile shadowed his lips. "No. I grew up in Glen Kerr, on Loch Lomond," he said. "One of four children born to Hamish and Mhairi MacKinnon."

"Four?"

He grinned, nodded. "Yep. And I was number four. I'm the youngest and, according to my brothers and sister, that's what's wrong with me." He essayed a sheepish grin.

"So you're the baby, then?" she asked, feeling her lips twitch. She nodded gravely. "Yep, that would definitely screw a guy up." She gave a wistful sigh. "It must have been nice having all those siblings though, right? Never a dull moment? Never at a loss for a playmate?"

"Never a clean towel," he interjected with a moan, leaning back in his chair. "Never any privacy." He paused and shot her a look. "All kidding aside, it was nice, and I appreciate it more the older I get. That said, there's no way in hell I could live with all of them."

"Live with them?"

"My parents live in the carriage house on the estate and my older brother and sister live in the manor house. They're all always together. It would unnerve me. Myself and my brother Cam, who has what he likes to call his rotting pile of ruin, are the only ones who left the nest, so to speak."

She felt her eyes widen. "Wow. That is a lot of to-getherness." Granted she missed having siblings and would love nothing better than a sister, but she wasn't sure she'd want to live with them. Isla liked her own space. "So when did you move to Lochawe? How long have you been building boats?"

Another one of those crooked smiles and he laughed softly. "Since I could float bark and attach a leaf as a sail," he said. "We always had a dinghy on the loch in front of the house and from the time I was old enough to sit in the boat, my dad would take me out. I loved being on the water, was amazed at how we could glide across the surface and drop anchor any where we wanted. Later, I became obsessed with early boat builders—how they'd built their ships—and even more obsessed with explorers and sailors. It takes a lot of courage to head out into open sea, to try to navigate something as vast and wonderful as the ocean. And being out there…" A faraway look lit his gaze. "There's nothing like it."

The passion in his voice was palpable, awe-inspiring. This was a man who knew his purpose, who was in love with his craft.

It was intensely attractive. Lord, help her.

"Sorry," he said. "I tend to get carried away."

She took a sip of her drink and tried to drag her gaze away from his mouth. She loved the way it moved when he spoke. "Don't apologize," she said. "Would that everyone could be so delighted with their job. Just think how much happier people would be, how the quality of their work would improve."

"True," he said, staring at her again, making her heart rate kick into an irregular rhythm. He seemed to shake himself. "Anyway, I went to university, studied engineering and nautical sciences, then combed the countryside to find the best boat builder in Scotland to apprentice with and found your father." He smiled, his eyes full of admiration. "He's the best, your father. Can put a boat together better than anyone I've ever seen. I owe him a lot."

His heart-felt sentiment made her throat grow tight. "He thinks a lot of you as well."

His gaze tangled significantly with hers, sucking the air out of her lungs. "He'd think a lot less of me if he knew what I was thinking right now."

Oy. The tops of her thighs caught fire at the innuendo in his tone.

"Come on," he said. "I'd better get you home…while I've got strength enough to leave you," he added under his breath.

ISLA STOOD AND PROMPTLY wobbled, so naturally—instinctively—he reached out to steady her. That touch, innocuous though it was, completely undermined all his good intentions. And he'd had them, he knew. He'd picked her up tonight knowing that he had to be careful, that he was playing with fire—Fergus's fire, he reminded himself, hoping his conscience could scream loud enough to pull him out of this quagmire of lust—and yet…she'd completely undone him.

Obvious qualities aside—like the fact that she was drop dead gorgeous—there was something about her, a goodness, for lack of a better description, that made her attractive on more than just a superficial level. If she'd been only physically attractive, he would have easily resisted.

But she was more than that. She was…creative and funny, witty and smart, vulnerable and sexy and, though he wasn't sure where this knowledge came from, lonely. It shadowed the light in her gaze, haunted her smile and made him desperately long to help her. It was presumptuous of him to even think he could and yet the impulse was there all the same. He wasn't any closer to knowing what had made her turn up here after all these years, but something told him that the melancholy he saw behind her smile had something to do with it. She was a puzzle, Fergus's daughter, a beautiful riddle he'd like nothing better to solve.

Preferably in a bed.

But he would not, he told himself. He'd get her home, then retreat to his own place. A little distance would ready him for tomorrow and then by the end of the day Fergus would be home and he could go on his merry way. The idea rang hollowly in his gut, a warning sound, but he dismissed it as a product of too much of a good time and too much alcohol.

"Whoa," he said, chuckling to lighten the moment. The sweet swell of her breast lay against his arm and her fruity scent swirled up his nose, momentarily stunning him. "Are you okay?"

She laughed and clung to him until she steadied. "The floor moved," she said, a frown in her voice. "It's been a long time since that's happened to me."

Because he was a stupid glutton for punishment, he wrapped his arm around her waist. "That ale will sneak up on you," he told her. "I should have warned you."

"I should have known better," she said. "I'm not much of a drinker. Alcohol loosens my tongue and I invariably say things that get me into trouble. Ooo, you smell good," she announced suddenly, leaning over to sniff his neck.

He gritted his teeth so hard he feared they'd crack. A line of gooseflesh raced down his spine.

"Oh, see?" she said with a weak giggle. "That's exactly what I'm talking about."

He opened her car door and helped her in, then reached across her and fastened her seat belt. She grew completely still and he paused, then looked over and realized her mouth was only an inch from his face, their noses practically touching.

She swallowed, the fine muscles in her throat working along the smooth column of her neck.

Fergus's daughter, Fergus's daughter, Fergus's daughter.

Scraping the dredges of his soul for a little more self-restraint, he determinedly clicked the belt into place, then withdrew and shut her door. He walked around the back of the truck because it was a longer route and she wouldn't see him trying to tear his hair out.

The short drive back up the hill felt like an eternity and by the time he'd shifted into Park and had come around to open her door, he felt like he'd aged a thousand years. He took her hand to help her out of the car and the simple contact somehow made the ground shift beneath his feet.

She gasped and her eyes twinkled. "Looks like I'm

not the only one who got carried away with the ale." She frowned. "You probably shouldn't have driven. It's a short enough walk."

"I'm fine," he said, shaken to the soles of his shoes. A finger at her back, he opened the gate and ushered her through, then followed her to the door. Porch light gilded her red hair and shined on the side of her face, casting the other in complete darkness. She pulled the key out of her purse and then turned to him.

"Thank you for taking me to dinner," she said. "I know that my father asked you to do it, but—"

"I didn't mind," he insisted. Quite the opposite, really.

"Nevertheless, regardless of your motivation, it was nice. I enjoyed myself." She grinned at him, her rosy mouth ripe and inviting. "You're quite good company." Her eyes widened. "Oops. There I go again."

He'd been called many things in his life, but good company had certainly never been one of them. As far as compliments went though, it was a damned fine one. "Thank you. Likewise," he said, staring down at her. She seemed closer. Had he moved? Had she? Did it matter? Dammit, he had to get out of here. If he didn't leave soon he didn't think he'd be able to at all. Siren, he thought. So damned tempting.

"So I'll see you in the morning, then? Say around eight?"

"Sounds good." She leaned forward and pressed a kiss to his cheek. He froze, felt that little kiss blast through him like a sonic boom. Need, longing, desire all tangled around his insides and knotted in his groin. He squeezed his eyes shut, shoved his hands into his pockets to keep from wrapping them around her and took a step back.

She was killing him—*absolutely killing him*—and being honorable had never been more difficult or less comfortable.

"I should go," he said with less conviction than he'd like, his gaze snagging hers. He really should. He should and yet…he couldn't.

She moistened her lips, her eyes heavy-lidded with a want he recognized because it was torturing him as well. "You should," she agreed. A beat slid to three, then, "But I don't want you to."

6

Isla let the comment hang between them and waited. She knew she was being shameless and could only credit the ale for a teensy bit of that, but dammit…she wanted to be irresistible. She wanted him to want her as much as she wanted him.

She just *wanted*. So very, very much.

Alec looked at her again and she watched his desire to be noble wage war against his desire for her, and she knew the exact instant when she'd won, when he surrendered. He backed her up against the door, braced his hands on both sides of her head and then moved in until he was a hairsbreadth from her mouth.

"Are you sure about that?"

Her heart pounded in her chest and anticipation tightened her nerves and she laughed softly. "More sure of that than anything else at the moment."

Male satisfaction clung to his smile and his lids dropped to half-mast. "Well, in that case…"

He closed the distance between them, pressing his lips against hers. If a kiss could be a color, she'd say this one was purple—it was dark and luscious, beautiful and sinfully thrilling. His lips clung to hers, molded, sampled and tasted and his tongue danced around her own, a mind-numbing wondrous game of seek and retreat. She felt the breath thin in her lungs, then leak out of her in a long, satisfied exhale. It was as though she'd been unwittingly looking for something…and found it right here, an unknown treasure she wasn't expecting.

He reached down and opened the door, never losing contact with her mouth, and then guided her inside. She framed his face with her hands, testing the feel of him with her greedy fingers, and pushed them into his hair. He answered in kind, tipping her head to give him better access to her mouth. He was hot and hard, his hands big and calloused from years of working with them and they felt delicious against her skin.

Skin that suddenly felt too tight, too hot, for her own body.

Her nipples beaded behind her bra and her breasts grew heavy. A muddled warmth flooded her womb and seeped into her panties and she could feel the center of her sex throbbing with every quickened, desperate beat of her heart. She moaned low in her throat and squirmed against him.

"Bed," he said simply, lifting her off the floor. She wrapped her arms around his neck once more, feasted on his mouth and let him carry her into her room. He set her down and shucked his shirt, revealing a chest that was splendidly muscled with whorls of dark hair around flat male nipples. Her shirt joined his on the floor, boots thumped to the carpet and the frantic whine of zippers punctuated their equally frantic kiss. He broke away long enough to put a condom on the nightstand, then covered his body with hers.

Sleek skin, supple muscle and bone. He smelled warm and musky with a tang of salt and the first feel of his bare flesh against her own was as thrilling as it was comforting. Despite not knowing him, there was a strange familiarity to his touch that she couldn't explain, couldn't rationalize, but made it all the more welcome.

He nuzzled her neck with his nose, skimmed kisses along her jaw line, then bent his dark head and pulled a pouting nipple into his hot mouth.

She moaned and bucked beneath him and he answered with a deft touch between her legs, stroking her clit while feeding at her breast. It was as though an invisible string were linked between the two and he was playing it like a musical instrument, pulling sounds from her she'd never imagined she'd make. She felt the first flash of orgasm quicken in her womb and gasped, then reached down and took him in hand.

Two could play at this game.

He was hot and hard, the silken skin slippery against her palm and she worked him slowly, reveling in her sudden power as he growled his approval against her breast.

Her ministrations had the desired effect and she felt him shift enough to get the condom. He drew back, his dark hair mussed, his gray eyes smoldering with heat, then he tore the package open with his teeth and quickly rolled it into place.

A nanosecond later he was poised between her thighs, nudging her entrance, the heavy weight of him feeling perfect—fated, destined, pre-ordained—against her. She felt like she was standing on a precipice and one touch from him would push her over the edge.

A strange look of wondering bewilderment on his beautiful face, he bent down and pressed his lips to hers, kissed her deeply, then slowly pushed into her.

The air whooshed out of her lungs as he filled her up, stretched her to make room for him, then he threaded his fingers through hers, anchored them over her head and drew back and plunged again.

The relief of having him inside of her, having him seated as fully and firmly as he could be, was so stark it made her release a long laughing sigh.

He drew back and looked at her, his lips quirked in an endearing grin. "My lovemaking amuses you? This is not the sort of response a man finds flattering."

Still smiling, she leaned forward and nipped at his shoulder, drew her legs back and squeezed her feminine muscles. She had the pleasure of watching his smile falter and a hiss slip past his lips. "Then perhaps you should try harder."

"Harder?" He thrust deeply. "You mean like this?"

She gasped, absorbing his thrusts, matching them with her own. "Oh, yeah," she said, her eyes all but rolling back in her head. "That'll do."

And five spectacular, well-aimed thrusts later, it did.

She shattered…and dimly decided that if kisses were purple, then orgasms were a kaleidoscope of color too intricate to describe.

And love? Love, if she were to hazard a guess, would be gray.

RED HAIR FANNED OUT against a pink pillow, mouth opened in a soundless scream of pleasure, neck arched away from the bed as greedy feminine muscles tightened around him…

Clearly he'd died and gone to heaven, Alec thought as he plunged deeper into Isla's hot little body. Nipples puckered like ripe raspberries sat atop the creamy globes of her breasts, begging for his kiss, and her thighs clamped tightly around his waist.

If this wasn't heaven, then he didn't know what was. He was mindless with sensation, could feel her in every cell of his body, with every beat of his heart. The first shock of awareness when he'd slid into her had practically liquefied his insides it had resonated so hard.

She didn't just feel good—she felt *right*.

She felt like every part of her had been made to fit perfectly against every part of him, and the sense of peace and homecoming when he'd seated himself fully into her was simply…beyond description.

Alec had been sexually active since he was seventeen—which was quite late according to his older brothers' teasing—and knew his way around a female body. He knew what to put where, which buttons to push, which parts to lick and which parts to suckle. He knew where to squeeze and where to massage and he knew when a girl was close to coming for him, when one was fully enjoying him. But all of that experience, that wealth of accumulated knowledge, paled in comparison to what was happening to him right now.

If being attracted to her had been beyond anything he'd ever encountered, then bedding her was even more so. He should have realized, should have known…

He hadn't been resisting this out of respect for his mentor, though admittedly that had been a part it.

No, he'd been resisting her because something had

told him that she was going to be different, that she was going to rock his world, turn it upside and set it on end.

He'd been resisting out of self-preservation.

But it was too late now. It was too late and he was too far gone.

He lifted her hips, angled deeper and rode her harder, could feel his balls slapping against her hot flesh, her feminine channel tightening around him with every determined, desperate thrust. She bent forward and touched her tongue to his nipple, lightly bit the nub and he didn't just come…

He exploded.

Release blasted through him, ricocheted along every vein, every muscle. His vision blackened around the edges, then blazed back into color and he drove deeper, putting the hardest part of him in the softest, deepest part of her. His toes dug into the mattress and she wrapped her arms around him, kissed his shoulder and held him tighter as he went suddenly weak, boneless.

Though there was precious little room on the twin bed, he rolled over, discarded the condom into a tissue he found on the nightstand, then tucked her up against his side.

Breathing heavily, her small hand lay against his ribs and she slung a smooth leg over his own. Contentment like he'd never known spread like butter over warm bread through him and he smiled and pressed a kiss against her hair.

He looked around the room, truly seeing it for the first time. It was pink, with lots of frilly girl things on the walls. Posters of unicorns and the like. It was obvious that Fergus had decorated it for her when she'd been a little girl and then left it, evidently not able to abandon the idea that she'd come back.

With a flash of premonition, he sincerely hoped he wouldn't make the same mistake.

He wondered again why she'd made the trip over now, but even though they'd just shared the most intimate act two people could physically, he was reluctant to ask her because it still felt too personal.

"Thank you for staying," she said. "I'm not usually so…forward," she managed, evidently struggling to find the right word.

He snorted. "Please," he deadpanned. "We all know American girls are easy."

She laughed, seemingly outraged, and whacked him on the chest. "No, they're not," she insisted. "It's a myth that's perpetuated thanks to poor television programming."

"And horny American girls whose heads are turned with a virile Scottish brogue."

"The brogue adds to your appeal," she admitted. "I love the way it sounds, the roll of the *r*'s."

"I like your accent, too," he told her. "It's soft and lilting, unhurried." He paused. "This is the first time I've ever seen this room," he remarked.

She hummed sleepily under her breath in response.

"Fergus always had the door shut when I was over."

"Alec?"

He loved the way she said his name, the breathy finish on the *c*. "Yes?"

"Keeping in mind that I mean this in the kindest, gentlest way possible…shut up."

He felt a chuckle break in his throat and held her tighter. "Right. Of course."

"G'night," she murmured, rubbing her cheek against his chest.

"Night."

7

"ARE YOU SURE we're allowed to be here?" Isla asked as Alec opened the gate to let her in.

"Of course," he told her. "Kilchurn is one of Scotland's most beloved ruins," he said. "As well as the most photographed, I believe. I've been coming here for years. It's a beautiful old place." Threading his fingers through hers as though it was as natural as breathing, he tugged her forward. Isla's heart gave a little squeeze.

This morning when she'd awoken it had been with this gorgeous Scot bellied up to her back, his big callused hand laid possessively over her breast. She'd felt him breathe, the soft rise and fall of his chest, and something about that had soothed her more than she could have ever imagined. She'd never been much of a snuggler, had always preferred her own space in bed, but she'd been contented in a way this morning that was completely new for her. For the first time in her life, she felt like she was in the right place at the right time, that she and destiny were on the same page.

It was ridiculous, she knew. She'd known him less than twenty-four hours and had behaved quite shockingly with him. By her standards, anyway. She'd lain awake this morning and tried to figure out why that was and, ultimately, off-the-charts attraction aside, it was because she felt safe with him. Why? Who knew? But she couldn't deny the absolute assurance she felt that he wouldn't deliberately hurt her. She swallowed.

But she'd hurt when she left here, Isla knew.

Already the thought of leaving made her feel anxious and sick in her stomach. And she hadn't even seen her father yet. No doubt it would only worsen then. As if sensing her unease, Alec squeezed her hand and she looked over at him and smiled.

Drops of mist clung to his dark head and eyelashes and his mouth was turned in an easy smile. Alec MacKinnon was comfortable without being cocky, at ease in his own skin, and that only added to his considerably lethal appeal. Though they'd showered together this morning and repeated last night's fun festivities—

Hot wet naked skin, muscled arms clamped around her belly as he pushed into her from behind, steam rising around them as she came, like poetic evidence of her climax...

—her belly gave a hard clench and warmth saturated her panties anew. Mercy, this man was like a drug, one that she was becoming addicted to.

"Do you want to make it to the castle?" he asked in a conversation tone.

She blinked. "I'm sorry?"

"If you want to make it to the castle, then you need to stop looking at me like that, otherwise I'm going to tackle you to the ground—where it's entirely possible we'll land in sheep shit—and I'll take you right here, damn the consequences."

Him taking her right here—minus the sheep shit, of course—was perfectly all right with her. She bit her lip, feigning contrition. "Sorry."

Another smile twitching over his beautiful lips, gray eyes twinkling with humor, he continued to lead the way. The small footpath led through a bit of underbrush and trees before opening up to a huge meadow dotted with sheep and thistles. The castle, which was sitting right up against Loch Awe, loomed large in front of them, stealing her breath. She paused, absorbing the scene. Mist hung over water that was smooth as glass and clung to the top of the castle and wove around the mountains. And all of it—every last breathtaking detail—was in duplicate, reflected back from the mirrored surface of the water.

Loch Awe indeed, Isla thought, as something strange and wonderful winged through her chest. She felt a bizarre connection to this place, to the air, the very earth. The fine hair on her arms stood on end, dotting her skin with gooseflesh, and she shivered as a hush of expectancy settled over her heart.

He squeezed her hand again. "Beautiful, isn't it?"

She nodded, unable to speak, and started toward the castle, desperate to explore. She was glad that they'd made an early start of it—unless she was mistaken, they were the only ones here.

Alec ushered her inside, where some of the soaring stone walls rose into turrets and some into beautiful sky. Huge empty fireplaces were carved out among the rock and you could still see the square holes where the beams and joists would have been to support the upper floors.

"This is incredible," she breathed. "Utterly incredible."

"Allow me to be your tour guide," he said, seemingly glad that she was enjoying herself. He cleared his throat. "The castle was built around 1450 by the first Lord of Glenorchy, Sir Colin Campbell. Originally, the castle was on a small island and would have been accessed through a low-lying causeway, but the water levels were altered in 1817 and thus connected it to the mainland."

She looked up at him and grinned, impressed. "You know your stuff."

He shrugged, and rubbed the back of his neck. "Scotland has a lot of history."

Didn't she know that? It was particularly incredible to consider that this castle was more than twice as old as her country. Certainly put things into perspective, that was for sure.

She pointed to a staircase. "Is it safe to go up there?"

"Safe if you're careful," he told her. "You have little feet for those little treads, so you should be all right." He nudged her forward. "Go on," he said. "I'll follow you."

"So that you can stare at my ass?"

He grinned. "That, too, but I was actually thinking that I could catch you if you fell, or at the very least, break your fall. I'd hate for you to break that pretty neck."

Startled that his unwitting first thought was for her safety, she paused and turned around, more touched than she could have imagined.

And she'd wondered why she'd felt safe with him?

But there were many ways to define safe and given the predatory look in his eye—one that thrilled her and made her toes curl in her boots—she suspected he had an ulterior motive for wanting her to climb those stairs.

ALEC'S INTENTIONS WEREN'T quite as noble as he'd like her to think they were. The castle was empty this time of the morning, with no one else here, and he wanted to take advantage of that.

By taking her.

He watched her shapely rear swing back and forth as she ascended the stairs and felt his dick swell with every mesmerizing sway. When she mounted the last tread and stepped into the small circular room, he whirled her around and caught the delighted "oh" from her mouth with his own. She instantly—gratifyingly—responded with a groan of pure delight and wrapped her arms around his neck. She was small and curvy with flesh where there should be flesh and she felt *wonderful* against him. The scent of her flooded his nostrils and he breathed her in, wanting nothing more than to eat her up. To lick and suck and lave and taste.

She framed his face with her hands, curving her palm along his jaw, his cheek and there was something reverent and poignant in the gesture, something that made his chest squeeze and a dart of panic land in his heart.

Oh, hell no, Alec thought, a sense of inevitable doom settling over him.

He bent low and ground his hips against her, telegraphing his intentions, and she gasped and clung tighter to him. Despite the cool morning temperatures, he was on fire. Literally burning up from the inside out. He backed her over toward a small rectangle window, then turned her around where she could appreciate the view of the loch below, the picture framed in the non-existent window.

Knowing what he wanted—what he needed, God help him—she made quick work of her jeans, sliding them down over her hips, grabbed hold of the stone edge with her hands, then spread her legs and backed up against him.

He was ready for her.

Condom in place, he thrust up and slid home. She winced with pleasure, tightened her feminine muscles around him and arched her back. He swept her hair aside and found where neck met shoulder and kissed while he plundered her sweet, dark heat. Harder and faster and faster still, he plunged in and out of her, their lovemaking punctuated by the occasional bleating of a sheep.

"Alec," she cried, her breath coming in little labored puffs. "I need— Oh, please—"

He knew exactly what she needed. He reached around and fingered the swollen nub hidden at the top of her sex, a secret treasure of sensation designed to give her more, to take her higher. She purred for him, made a keening noise that impossibly made him harder, made his balls draw up, and everything inside of him prepared for climax, for that one brilliant shining moment when he'd come apart inside of her, "the little death" as the French liked to say.

He could feel her squirming against him, tightening around him and when he knew she was about to shatter, he leaned forward and whispered in her ear. "Look," he said, indicating the view out the window. Her country. Her home. *"Look."*

She did…and shattered for him.

Three hard thrusts later, his throat raw from the scream that had torn from him—a guttural sound that had never passed his lips before—he came, too.

Breathing heavily, reluctant to withdraw, he held her tighter and rested his head next to hers on her shoulder, sharing the view. Sharing the moment. Sharing the magic.

And he knew in that instant that he'd never be the same, that he was going to be like Fergus…that he'd always be waiting for her.

8

STILL SHAKEN FROM the turret experience—even though it had been hours ago—Isla wandered among the Giants' Graves, a mystical place on the Isle of Arran. They'd made the journey by Alec's boat—seeing him on the water had certainly been an experience—and then on foot. It had been a lot of walking, first to Glenashdale Falls—simply stunning—and then up the steep two-hundred-sixty-five step staircase cut directly into the hillside up to the Giants' Graves. The graves weren't actually giants', of course, but rather referred to the huge monolithic stones—an estimated five thousand years old—that marked the ground where the earliest people were buried.

The place was beautiful, but almost eerie, for a lack of better description. She slid a finger over a stone, feeling the moss, and cast a covert look at Alec. He'd been different since visiting Kilchurn, but she couldn't pinpoint the exact change. He was just as happy, just as courteous, just as attentive and yet she knew something had altered.

Of course, she'd went through some adjustments, as

well. Honestly, when she remembered the view from that turret—the feast before her eyes—combined with the feast of her senses—him, hot, hard and wonderful, and so very much alive, pushing in and out of her, the rush of sensation whirling through her and then his "Look," command whispered gruffly in that beautiful raw brogue—it had almost been too much, too good, too intense.

She still couldn't exactly identify what precisely had shifted inside of her, she only knew that it had.

"Your dad should be arriving soon," Alec said. He smiled, but it didn't quite reach his eyes. "I don't think I've ever heard him as excited as when I told him that you were here. He was over the moon."

Isla swallowed. "It's been too long."

The grin turned droll. "Judging by the fact that your bedroom is still decorated in unicorns and butterflies, I'd say so."

"I was surprised to find that he hadn't redecorated," she admitted. She fondled a fern and swallowed. "And a little relieved, too. It's nice to know that he didn't give up on me."

Alec glanced up, seemingly startled. "You're his daughter, Isla. Of course, he'd never give up on you."

She grimaced. "Then he had more faith in me than I had in him," she said, feeling a lump well in her throat. "I wouldn't have blamed him, you know. I can blame my mother for my lack of visits when I was younger—I was underage and without funds. But after college..." She heaved a long sigh. "I don't know. Money was tight, though I know he would have bought me a ticket, but it was just easier to stay home, to keep my mother from freaking out. If I ever mentioned wanting to come over, she was always ready to remind me that 'flights weren't just one way' and that 'if he'd loved us enough, he would have come to us.'"

Looking alternately angry and pitying, he took a step toward her. "Isla—"

"I know now that that was only her bitterness talking," she said. "But I'll admit that I was always afraid that I'd been an inconvenience, unwanted maybe, and it was just easier to stay away, to not risk getting hurt."

And it was true, she realized with a sudden burst of insight. She'd always been afraid that her father might not *really* want her around, would begrudge her coming over and interrupting his life.

Alec was quiet for a long time, his jaw flexed. She could feel his tension pinging her like sonar. After a moment, he looked up at her. "I'm not going to say anything unkind about your mother, though I will say that she sounds rather manipulative."

She was that, Isla had to admit.

"But I will say that I've known your father for a long time and I think I know him about as well as anybody can ever really know a person." He paused. "And he's grieved over not seeing you. I don't know why your parents divorced, I don't know who was at fault," he said through gritted teeth, "but I do know that he loves you with all that he has and would welcome you into *your* home here anytime you'd like to visit it." He grunted, looked away. "That room of yours speaks for itself, doesn't it?"

It had, actually, and had convinced her more than anything her father could have said, that was for sure. It had been proof positive that he'd been waiting for her, that despite the fact that she was grown and hardly saw him, she was still his little girl.

Her gaze slid to Alec once more. Light filtered greenly through the trees, casting him in a strange glow. He wore a navy blue sweater, a pair of jeans and boots. His coffee-colored hair was mussed from the wind and had put a bit of pink on his cheeks. In practical terms he was almost a stranger and yet she *knew* him and in more than the biblical sense.

She knew the shape of his smile, the twinkle of humor in his eyes. She knew that he was happiest when he was working with his hands, that he took pride in his craft. She knew that he loved the water and his freedom on it, that he admired wit and intelligence. She knew that he liked cream in his tea, preferred gooseberry jam to orange marmalade and that he was the kind of man who would send her up a set of stairs first so that he could catch her if she fell.

He was good and true and wonderful and, while she didn't think she could possibly be in love with him yet, she knew that she would be eventually.

And the idea of leaving him, of saying goodbye to him and to her father and to Scotland was more painful than she would have ever, ever imagined.

"We should go," Alec told her. He slung an arm around her shoulder and pressed a kiss to her temple. "When's your flight again?"

She swallowed. "Tomorrow evening, at eight." So soon? Could that possibly be right? But she wasn't ready— She didn't—

"Your dad will want to see you off," he said, then turned her toward him and slid a finger longingly over her cheek. His gaze raked over her face, seemingly memorizing the lines. "So if it's all right with you, I'll go ahead and collect my farewell kiss now."

Her heart gave a painful squeeze as he lowered his mouth to hers. His lips were warm and insistent, careful but thorough, and there was a desperate undertone that she not only understood, but felt as well because this, sadly, was the end of whatever this had been.

And it couldn't be more because they lived on different continents and she knew, much like her father, he was as much a part of Scotland as the stones around them.

Could she move? Could she come here? What about her mother? Her animals? Her business? Could she leave it all behind to make a life here? She honestly didn't know.

But if goodbyes had a color, Isla thought, then they were definitely blue.

ALEC HEARD THE COMPANY truck lumber up the hill and watched Isla bolt from the table, out the door, through the gate and directly into her father's arms.

"Ah, lass, it's good to see ye," Fergus told her, his voice oddly strangled as he held her tight. "If I'd known you were coming I'd have met you at the airport," he said. "We'd have made a proper visit out of it."

"It's proper enough now that you're here," Isla said, drawing back to look at him. She was smiling from ear to ear and happy tears slid over her cheeks. She slipped her arm through his and they made their way through the gate.

"Fergus," Alec said, feeling a bit weird greeting his friend knowing that he'd had sex with the man's daughter three times in the last twenty-four hours, twice under his own roof. "Glad to see you made it back safely."

Beaming at him, Fergus nodded his graying red head. "Thanks, Alec. I'm assuming you took care of my girl?"

That was one way of putting it, he supposed. Alec's gaze flitted briefly to Isla's suddenly guilty one, and he nodded at his old friend. "I think so," he said. "But you'll have to ask her."

"He was a wonderful host, Dad." She smiled, but it didn't fit on her face just right. "We've had a great time."

"Excellent," Fergus boomed. "Glad to hear it."

Because they had so little time to themselves, Alec knew he needed to take his leave, but was reluctant to do so. He didn't want to walk away from her, instinctively knowing he was going to feel her absence. Still, he must. He made himself look at her, made his mouth shape the words. "Isla, it's been a pleasure getting to you know. I hope you won't wait so long to visit next time."

Her eyes a little bright, a little startled, she swallowed and nodded. "I won't, thank you. For everything," she added.

And with that, he strolled through the gate and over to his own house. Mackie greeted him with an enthusiastic hand lick as he sank into his chair. The house was quiet, familiar, exactly the same.

And yet it wasn't anymore.

Because he had changed.

Another turn on the water was in order, Alec thought. And he sincerely hoped it would provide the therapy he needed.

THE NEXT MORNING Isla stood over her little twin bed, her suitcase open, and methodically, with a heart that had turned to lead, stowed her things. She dashed a tear from her cheek as she closed the top and pulled the zipper into place.

"I suppose we need to update this room," her father said from the doorway, startling her. "You're always going to be my little girl, but I suspect you've outgrown butterflies and unicorns."

She turned to look at him and felt her smile wobble. "I don't want you to change a thing, Dad. I love this room just as it is."

Her gruff old father passed a weathered hand over his equally weathered and lined face. "It's been nice having you in it. I know you've got your own place in the States now," he said. "But this is your home, too." He paused, seemed to choose his words carefully. "Whatever you may have been told or led to believe, it's always been your home and it always will be."

And that was as close to maligning her mother as he was going to get, she knew. He wouldn't say anything derogatory about his ex-wife out of respect for *her*. Would that her mother had bestowed the same courtesy, Isla thought. She might have spent a whole lot more time with him. But you couldn't un-ring a bell and what was done was done. There was nothing to do now but move forward.

And right now, she had to put one foot in front of the other enough to get her home. She had responsibilities. As much as she might like to stay here with her father, to explore her new relationship with Alec—the thought of him made her heart hurt and her body ache—she couldn't just abandon her life and start over here.

At least…not right now.

Isla hesitated, looked up at her father. "You really mean that, don't you?"

He nodded without hesitation. "I do."

"And if I moved in with a menagerie of pets? What then?"

"I like animals," her father said, a glimmer of a smile on his mouth. "You've met Ahab."

"I've got two dogs, two cats and four birds," she told him. "Provided I could bring them all over. I think with proper paperwork I could get the cats and dogs in. I'm not sure about the birds," she added, frowning.

"Lass, you could move Noah's whole bloody ark in here and as long as you came with it, I'd be thrilled. Are you truly considering it? Would you really move to Scotland?"

Yes, she would, Isla suddenly realized. As far as her business was concerned, she could just as easily work from here as she could from Georgia. And provided she could square away her pets and find someone to take over her fostering, she would definitely move to Scotland. She loved it here—and was loved here—and wanted to make up for lost time. Would her mother rant and rail? Yes, but not for long because she was too cheap to pay for long distance. She'd get over it and, with any luck, she'd have a new husband to help her do it.

Isla nodded, more certain than she'd ever been about anything in her life.

Her father grinned at her. "Alec must have shown you a real right time here in our little town," he said.

She blushed. "He's quite nice."

"He is that," her father agreed, a knowing twinkle in his eye and she got the distinct impression that he was quite pleased with himself. She inwardly gasped and her gaze met her father's once more.

"What?" he asked innocently.

Nah, she thought. Surely he hadn't asked Alec to escort her because he was trying to do some amateur match-making? He couldn't have known that they'd—

"Well, come on," her father said, hurrying her along. "The sooner you get everything squared away over there, the sooner you can get back." He hugged her again, squeezing the breath from her lungs.

Giddy, and confident that her feet were firmly—finally—on the right path, Isla looked up at her dad and smiled. "Thank you for waiting on me."

He grinned. "Always, lass, always."

"And, Dad?"

"Yes?

"Let's keep this between us."

Another knowing grin. "Ah," he said. "Another surprise, eh?"

Yes, she thought. And she sincerely hoped he'd like it.

Three weeks later...

ALEC WAS GLAD that Fergus was in an excellent mood because it off-set his own foul one. He'd been in a miserable funk—to the point that one of the guys had asked him if he was on his period—ever since Isla had left. Though he wouldn't have thought it was possible to become so attached to a person in little more than twenty-four hours, he most definitely had. The color had leached from his world, leaving it much bleaker and drearier than it had ever been in his life. He couldn't say that he was in love with her—what did he know of love?—but he knew he cared enough about her that there was an ache because of her absence that he couldn't seem to soothe, a hole in the spot she'd occupied, however briefly, that he couldn't properly fill.

And he tried.

Mostly with ale, he'd admit, but he had made an effort and that was the important thing.

Fergus was whistling tunelessly, a happy smile on his face, with an occasional eye toward the road. He'd talked to someone on his mobile phone—evidently Isla had finally convinced him to get one—and seemed extraordinarily jolly.

It annoyed the hell out of him.

A moving truck lumbered over the rise and Fergus stilled, a wide smile breaking over his face. He looked back over at Alec, then started making his way toward his house, which was exactly where the moving truck was going.

A prickle of awareness nudged Alec's belly.

A happy Fergus plus a moving truck could only equal one thing.

Isla.

He narrowed his eyes, trying to pull the cab of the truck more into focus and his heart began to pound when he recognized a flash of long, curly red hair.

Alec dropped his tools and took off up the hill, passing Fergus in the process.

"Hey!" Fergus called.

He felt a bit bad overtaking the old man, but he couldn't seem to help himself. He needed to see her, to touch her, to prove that his mind wasn't playing tricks on him.

The truck rolled to a stop and he skidded up next to the passenger door and watched as she climbed down out of the cab, a tentative smile on her face.

"Surprise," she said.

Surprise? *Surprise?*

Whooping for joy, Alec scooped her up and whirled her around, as a wheezing Fergus finally made it up to the house. "You and your surprises," he said, pressing a kiss against her sweet lips. "Does this mean what I think this means?" he asked, his gaze searching hers.

"Put her down, lad," Fergus grumbled. "That's my daughter you're man-handling and mooning over."

True enough, Alec thought. Because he was over the moon for her.

She nodded tentatively. "Are you happy?" she asked.

"That depends," he said. "Are you here for good?"

"I am."

"Then I am *ecstatic,*" he said, kissing her again.

"What you are is in the way," Fergus told him. "Let me hug my daughter."

"In a minute," Alec told him. "She's my surprise, after all."

Isla drew back, her gaze caressing his face, a fond smile on her lips. "Oh, yeah," she said. "Love is definitely gray."

He frowned. "What?"

She grinned. "Nothing," she said. "I'm just thinking out loud."

"And in Scotland," he told her. "Right where you belong."

Epilogue

"—I'M GLAD that all of our boys have found their better halves, Mhairi," Hamish MacKinnon said. "I'm just wondering how all three of them ended up with American girls, that's all. What's wrong with the Scottish lasses?"

Genevieve overheard her mother murmur something soothing and then say the one word guaranteed to settle her meddling father—grandchildren.

"Seriously, Mhairi? You think they'll start so soon? Well, of course I know we didn't plan any of ours, but—"

This was bordering on the more-than-she-needed-to-know territory, Genevieve thought, shooting her father a glance.

He flushed and cleared his throat. "We'll talk about this more when I get home."

Genevieve didn't know what her father was marveling over. She'd met every one of her future sister-in-laws and found them all extremely charming and perfectly suited to each of her brothers. And she hoped her mother was right, that they would produce grandchildren quickly.

She'd love to be an aunt. She'd spoil them rotten and buy them sweets and do all the indulgent things aunts were allowed to do.

"Well," her father said after he'd hung up the phone, darting her an uncomfortable look. "I don't have a prayer in hell in getting any one of them to take over now."

She hummed under her breath, and continued to peruse the file he'd asked her to look over.

"It's for the best really," her father went on. "Not one of them has half the heart for it that you do. The company couldn't be in better hands."

Genevieve stilled and looked up at her father.

Blushing, he cleared his throat again and then finally quirked a brow. "I've been a bit of a fool, haven't I? Waiting on those boys when you've been here all along. My bright little shadow, always my second in command." He smiled wanly. "I'm surprised that you've held your tongue. I hope I haven't disappointed you too terribly, Genevieve. That was never my intent. Of course the company is yours to take over if you want it. If not, we can hire someone. Either way, I'm tired. I want to spend what's left of my life doting on your mother and bouncing those future grandchildren on my knee. What do you say?"

Genevieve sprang from her chair and flung herself into her father's arms. She was overjoyed, elated and otherwise beside herself. Recognition. At last. "I'll make you proud, Dad," she said, hugging him tightly.

"Oh, lass," her father told her, his voice thick. "You already have." He drew back and wiped a tear from her cheek and smiled. "You're not planning on marrying an American, too, are you?"

She chuckled. "Nope," she said.

"Excellent," he said with a relieved nod. "That's good to hear."

Genevieve grinned. "He's Irish."

* * * * *

Harlequin Blaze

COMING NEXT MONTH

Available June 28, 2011

#621 BY INVITATION ONLY
Lori Wilde, Wendy Etherington, Jillian Burns

#622 TAILSPIN
Uniformly Hot!
Cara Summers

#623 WICKED PLEASURES
The Pleasure Seekers
Tori Carrington

#624 COWBOY UP
Sons of Chance
Vicki Lewis Thompson

#625 JUST LET GO…
Harts of Texas
Kathleen O'Reilly

#626 KEPT IN THE DARK
24 Hours: Blackout
Heather MacAllister

You can find more information on upcoming
Harlequin® titles, free excerpts and more at
www.HarlequinInsideRomance.com.

HBCNM0611

REQUEST YOUR FREE BOOKS!
2 FREE NOVELS PLUS 2 FREE GIFTS!

Harlequin *Blaze*™

red-hot reads!

YES! Please send me 2 FREE Harlequin® Blaze® novels and my 2 FREE gifts (gifts are worth about $10). After receiving them, if I don't wish to receive any more books, I can return the shipping statement marked "cancel." If I don't cancel, I will receive 6 brand-new novels every month and be billed just $4.24 per book in the U.S. or $4.71 per book in Canada. That's a saving of at least 15% off the cover price. It's quite a bargain. Shipping and handling is just 50¢ per book in the U.S. and 75¢ per book in Canada.* I understand that accepting the 2 free books and gifts places me under no obligation to buy anything. I can always return a shipment and cancel at any time. Even if I never buy another book, the two free books and gifts are mine to keep forever.

151/351 HDN FC4T

Name	(PLEASE PRINT)

Address	Apt. #

City	State/Prov.	Zip/Postal Code

Signature (if under 18, a parent or guardian must sign)

Mail to the **Reader Service:**
IN U.S.A.: P.O. Box 1867, Buffalo, NY 14240-1867
IN CANADA: P.O. Box 609, Fort Erie, Ontario L2A 5X3

Not valid for current subscribers to Harlequin Blaze books.

Want to try two free books from another line?
Call 1-800-873-8635 or visit www.ReaderService.com.

* Terms and prices subject to change without notice. Prices do not include applicable taxes. Sales tax applicable in N.Y. Canadian residents will be charged applicable taxes. Offer not valid in Quebec. This offer is limited to one order per household. All orders subject to credit approval. Credit or debit balances in a customer's account(s) may be offset by any other outstanding balance owed by or to the customer. Please allow 4 to 6 weeks for delivery. Offer available while quantities last.

Your Privacy—The Reader Service is committed to protecting your privacy. Our Privacy Policy is available online at www.ReaderService.com or upon request from the Reader Service.

We make a portion of our mailing list available to reputable third parties that offer products we believe may interest you. If you prefer that we not exchange your name with third parties, or if you wish to clarify or modify your communication preferences, please visit us at www.ReaderService.com/consumerschoice or write to us at Reader Service Preference Service, P.O. Box 9062, Buffalo, NY 14269. Include your complete name and address.

USA TODAY *bestselling author B.J. Daniels
takes you on a trip to Whitehorse, Montana,
and the Chisholm Cattle Company.*

RUSTLED

Available July 2011 from Harlequin Intrigue.

As the dust settled, Dawson got his first good look at the rustler. A pair of big Montana sky-blue eyes glared up at him from a face framed by blond curls.

A woman rustler?

"You have to let me go," she hollered as the roar of the stampeding cattle died off in the distance.

"So you can finish stealing my cattle? I don't think so." Dawson jerked the woman to her feet.

She reached for the gun strapped to her hip hidden under her long barn jacket.

He grabbed the weapon before she could, his eyes narrowing as he assessed her. "How many others are there?" he demanded, grabbing a fistful of her jacket. "I think you'd better start talking before I tear into you."

She tried to fight him off, but he was on to her tricks and pinned her to the ground. He was suddenly aware of the soft curves beneath the jean jacket she wore under her coat.

"You have to listen to me." She ground out the words from between her gritted teeth. "You have to let me go. If you don't they will come back for me and they will kill you. There are too many of them for you to fight off alone. You won't stand a chance and I don't want your blood on my hands."

"I'm touched by your concern for me. Especially after you just tried to pull a gun on me."

"I wasn't going to shoot you."

Dawson hauled her to her feet and walked her the rest of the way to his horse. Reaching into his saddlebag, he pulled out a length of rope.

"You can't tie me up."

He pulled her hands behind her back and began to tie her wrists together.

"If you let me go, I can keep them from coming back," she said. "You have my word." She let out an unladylike curse. "I'm just trying to save your sorry neck."

"And I'm just going after my cattle."

"Don't you mean your boss's cattle?"

"Those cattle are mine."

"*You're* a Chisholm?"

"Dawson Chisholm. And you are…?"

"Everyone calls me Jinx."

He chuckled. "I can see why."

*Bronco busting, falling in love…it's all in a day's work.
Look for the rest of their story in*

RUSTLED

*Available July 2011 from Harlequin Intrigue
wherever books are sold.*